Echoes of Balance

The Ways Trilogy, Book 1

CALLY RYANNE

Echoes of Balance

REUTS PUBLICATIONS

First Edition
First Printing, 2013

Cover design by Ashley Ruggirello
Cover art © 2013 Anettfrozen/Serialkillerstock/Dewfooter

ISBN: 978-0-9896499-0-2

REUTS Publications
www.REUTS.com

Printed in the United States of America

For Lauren, first reader of all my middle school scribbles.

PROLOGUE

"Calypso, we have no choice," Marcus scolded.

"There is always a choice!" Calypso spat, standing quickly from the small table.

"The Ways are very clear about what's going on, about what we need to do."

"I don't care, Marcus!" Calypso hissed, crossing her arms over her chest as she moved to the window. "The Ways are not always right. There are other options! I've spoken to *her*, and she—"

"That's blasphemy," Marcus said, cutting off his wife. "I thought we agreed that you would end contact with that . . . that creature."

Calypso said nothing as she stared at the menacing clouds gathering outside. They had been forming for days, growing and swirling in the distance. And now they were here, moving closer and closer.

Marcus sighed, gesturing to the set of whirring silver instruments on the table. They were skewed unnaturally, as if they would fall apart at any moment. "You can't argue with them, Calypso."

"They don't speak of us!" she whispered, crossing back to the table.

"No, they speak of a new power disrupting the balance," Marcus replied, trying to keep his voice quiet.

"Why, then, must we remove ourselves?" Calypso demanded, sliding back into the chair next to him. "Why not find this power, eliminate it . . . ?"

"We are not the only Naimei."

"They're our *children*, Marcus," Calypso whispered, choking out a sob.

Marcus placed an arm around her shoulders. "They're not just *our* children. Alexei and Rodin will leave, too, and Nicolai. Piotr."

"It's easier for them!" Calypso cried, shrugging off her husband's attempt to console her. "Their children are grown. They all stopped aging long ago."

"Same as Mikhail," Marcus retorted.

"But, Chloe . . . she's so young . . ."

"Mikhail can care for his sister."

Calypso sniffed. "He's not ready."

Marcus gave her shoulders a squeeze. "He will become ready."

"Momma?" asked a quiet voice from the doorway.

Calypso hurriedly wiped her eyes with the back of her hand. "Yes, baby."

"I can't sleep," the little girl whined. Her silky-smooth, dark hair was mussed from tossing and turning. Her big, startling blue eyes stood out against her tanned skin.

"I'll come tuck you in, baby," Calypso cooed, rising from her seat.

Marcus grabbed her arm. When she turned, he mouthed, "And then, we have to go."

Calypso gave a terse, minute nod before turning a watery smile to her daughter.

The sound of rain echoed off the terracotta roof as the once subtle tap grew to a furious hammer. Calypso clasped her daughter's hand as the sky outside opened up, swallowing the small house in its downpour.

ONE

The forest that bordered the sleepy town of Molten was utterly still. No sounds of small animals scuttling in the underbrush; no soft chirping of birds in the distance.

The silence, she realized with a frown, was unnerving. Absently, she drew her left arm, laden in bandages, closer to her torso. Her right hand itched for the silver gleam at her side. There should never be absolute silence in the forest.

She squinted into the predawn darkness, scanning with a quick, experienced gaze. Somewhere ahead and slightly off to the left, a twig popped.

She froze.

Another branch snapped.

Her fingertips grazed the smooth hilt of her weapon as the underbrush exploded into the massive, shaggy form of a bear. Caught off guard, she rolled out of the way, barely escaping before the beast stood where she had.

The animal turned a mouthful of teeth toward her and released a guttural snarl. She crouched low to the ground, still wearing the solemn expression she'd had while walking. The bear, formidable and fierce, was a threat, but hardly the one she'd been expecting.

Slowly, she raised the hand holding the knife. Pinning the handle to her palm with her thumb, she waved her fingers vaguely above the hilt. Her lips silently formed the shapes of ancient words.

A glazed look crossed the beast's eyes. It shook its head experimentally from side to side, sniffing at the air. Then it simply turned, ambling off into the underbrush as mysteriously—though much more contentedly—as it had come.

For a long moment, she didn't move. Beads of sweat gathered on her previously clean brow as she waited for her breathing to return to normal.

Laughter rang out from the foliage behind her. She closed her eyes and sighed, "Alex."

"Chloe," the voice confirmed, followed by the rustle of leaves as a pale, dark-haired young man slid neatly to the ground from one of the lower branches. "It's good to see you're still on top of your game, Cousin."

Chloe rose to her feet, swiping at her besmudged wardrobe. "It's not necessary to test me every time you make your way back into town, Alex."

He waved one hand lazily, as if trying to banish her comment. "Of course it is. Mikhail tells me you're busy playing vampire hunter—who knows what else you're getting up to?"

"Was," she grunted. Now that her cousin had revealed himself, it was easy to feel the pulse of his more-than-human aura around her. She had been stupid not to notice it before. But, of course, that's what she got for so rarely using her abilities.

"Excuse me?"

"Was. Was playing vampire hunter." Her eyes flickered to her bandaged arm before darting back up.

Alex arched his eyebrow. "Rus fixed you?"

She shrugged. "He put the bone shards back in place. Said it has to set, though."

"Well, good. You can heal and then get back to activities more *becoming* of our kind. Like studying the Ways. Maybe then, you would already know why I'm here."

Her eyes narrowed. "The Naimei have always been fighters."

Alex let out a bark of laughter. "By necessity and breeding, not by trade! The Ways are our true calling. You know that."

Chloe rolled her eyes. Oh, the Ways. She remembered them well; they were her most hated childhood lesson. A mixture of science, oracles, and magic, they were the scales and balances that defined the world, pointing the way to harmony or chaos. She had spent years trying to avoid them, but only the Naimei could channel their magic and ensure the balance of the universe was maintained.

She felt something akin to guilt settling in her stomach. Her cousin was right; she should have at least *attempted* to follow the Ways. Especially now that she had given up her more thrilling sideline.

"Hunting can help right the Ways," she offered sullenly. "Most of the vampires were about to out themselves to humans."

Alex snorted. "You might have saved a few humans some trauma, maybe, if that makes you feel better. But somehow, I doubt the lowlifes you were taking out had any vast impact on the universe, Chloe."

She shrugged again, picking at a few stray threads unraveling from her bandages, careful of the knife still in her hand.

Lowlifes.

That brought up another issue entirely—the issue that had made her stop hunting—but it wasn't something she was ready to discuss. Especially with Alex.

As if sensing her tension, Alex's tone softened. "Do you want to walk and talk? Your house isn't far, right?"

She nodded in response and slipped the knife back into the slender sheath at her side.

They walked in silence, the soft sounds of the forest slowly returning. Birds chirped as the early morning sun peeked over the horizon. Squirrels darted through the treetops, claws scratching the branches as they chattered to the waking birds. It was calming, and for a while, Chloe was content to simply listen. But after the third minute of nature ambiance, she felt compelled to speak.

"So . . . you've seen Mikhail?"

It was not uncommon for a Naimei to move often—imbalances in the world could begin anywhere, after all. But her brother—he was especially restless. Maybe because he was especially driven. Not that he'd always been that way.

He, too, had abhorred the use of the Ways, and if family rumor was anything to go on, his rebellion had been much greater than her own. She imagined he'd amassed the scores of tattoos and snaking scars that wrapped his arms during his Lost Time, but they never talked about it. Especially after their parents Vanished and he'd been put in charge of her.

After that, he'd thrown himself into his studies as thoroughly as he had thrown himself into rebelling from them. Before long, he was moving constantly from one world-saving task to another. Occasionally, he would seek her out. But only occasionally.

The visits came with thrilling tales of his antics: seizing ancient tomes detailing dangerous magic; battling over-ambitious supernaturals; tracking down unsuspecting humans with latent magical abilities.

They also came with him leaving again.

As a child, she'd stood in the doorway of whatever relative was currently housing her, watching as he gathered books and tools and strode toward the door. He would pause, kneel to tap her chin with two knuckles, and then walk right past her tiny frame.

Following the Ways, she supposed.

"Yeah, he stopped by," Alex responded, breaking Chloe's reverie. "On his way to Germany, I think. Something has the shifters out there plenty nervous. I'm surprised he didn't stop by to see you, what with . . . well." His eyes traveled down to the cast on her arm.

She frowned at him. "I didn't tell him."

Alex arched his brow again. An infuriating look, really, with all of its implied judgment.

"He's just really busy, alright? I didn't want to bother him."

"How *did* you do that to your arm?" Alex asked carefully.

"Lost a fight," she said.

It was the understatement of the year. She could have won, had she not been . . . surprised.

She'd been in the forested area she always patrolled—the perfect triangle between the heart of the city, the edge of the forest proper, and the beginnings of suburbia. It was an unlikely place to find a dangerous creature, but the proximity of the area to human settlements meant she had to check. All it would take was one rogue vampire, unconcerned with safety or secrecy—and boom. A massacre in minutes.

She had stopped in a clearing just before dawn, pausing for a moment to revel in how quiet the night had been.

And then the girl had stumbled into view.

Disoriented, growling, blood dripping from her mouth; there'd been no question she was a new vampire—the most dangerous kind. If not carefully watched, there was no telling the damage they could do. And this one had definitely done damage.

But it was not the newborn vampire that had shattered her arm; she had been quick, simple work. Though strong, new vampires had yet to learn control over their more powerful bodies, losing all sense of themselves as the change overtook them. Like puppies tripping over their own legs. No, it wasn't until she was cleaning her knife in the dewy grass that she'd realized the girl wasn't alone.

The wail that had come from the treeline was unmistakably one of grief. The second vampire darted out of the shadows faster than any human could have moved. Kneeling next to the fallen girl, he'd fixed Chloe with a mournful stare that still burned in her mind.

His anguish had surprised her. The idea that a creature she'd disregarded, hunted, and hated could feel pain like that, could feel compassion and love, had felt foreign and unpleasant in the pit of her stomach.

She'd been trying to wrap her head around that new moral quandary when the vampire attacked. She hadn't even had time to brace herself before he'd grabbed her, slamming her into a tree, cracking the bark in a way that would have cracked ribs had she been human.

He'd seized her left arm before she could recover, squeezing as he yelled over the loss of his companion. She'd felt each fragment of bone as it drifted painfully out of place.

She'd only managed to get him off her long enough to escape by sheer luck. Thinking herself away, she'd disappeared from that forest clearing and reappeared in the closest safe place—her cousin's doorstep. By the time he'd dragged her inside, she could barely see from the pain, much less the exertion of using her powers.

A human doctor would have been at a loss to fix the damage done to her limb. But the healing powers of the Naimei—another tedious art she'd only ever partially committed to—had allowed her cousin to fix her. He'd spent a feverish six hours bent over her mangled appendage, and it had still taken her two days to get past the pain to the point she could go back into the world, to return home.

But thankfully, Alex didn't press further, simply accepting her lost-fight story at face value in a very uncharacteristic fashion. She assumed he thought she'd given up hunting because of her injury, and, though embarrassing, she was more willing to let him think that than tell him the truth:

She no longer felt comfortable killing beings that could mourn, no matter how rogue or wild they may have become.

"We're here," she said, more softly than she meant to.

They pushed through a patch of berry bushes into a small, overgrown yard. Chloe's tension eased as her boots met the too-tall grass. She was home.

Her modest house, set in the middle of the foliage and crawling with ivy, was situated at the tip of the forest triad, farthest from the wilderness and right on the edge of downtown Molten. Just on the other side of the park were some of her pre-ferred haunts: a few coffee shops, some restaurants, an old and dusty bookstore she felt strangely attached to. Though not a home she'd ever grown up in, she had instantly chosen it as her favorite when Mikhail bequeathed it and several more of their parents' properties to her after she had stopped aging.

The interior was just as cozy as the vine-wrapped exterior. The walls were painted with soft hues of blue, green, and yellow. The furniture, though well-worn and sun-faded, was overstuffed and inviting.

Bookshelves chock full of old, thick tomes with curious titles, some in languages that were barely recognizable, lined the living room. Strange sculptures, odd knick-knacks, and decorated box-es filled with mysterious instruments nestled among them.

Alex headed for the shelves as soon as they walked in the door. Chloe went for the large, wooden table that straddled the kitchen and living room. It was a thick, knobby thing with chairs to match. She pulled one out and sat down as her cousin blew a fine layer of dust from the lid of a box.

"Honestly, Chloe," he muttered as he made his way to the table, "you really open it that rarely?"

She kicked at a scuff-mark on the floor, making it worse. "The Ways don't change *that* often."

Alex let out an exasperated sigh. "Did you pay attention at all when you were first learning? The subtle changes are the *most* important."

"Good thing people like you devote their time to watching for them, then."

He rolled his eyes and set the box on the table. It was beautiful, elaborately-carved wood with a single metal clasp in the middle. The second he unlatched it, the lid sprang open, revealing three compartments. Within each was a collection of odd-looking instruments producing a low hum.

With deft, nimble hands, Alex removed the silver components and started assembling.

TWO

Assembled, the Ways were every bit as strange as they'd been in the box. There were no visible screws or supports to hold them, but hold they did. Large, polished spheres intermixed with the silver instruments, delicate engravings laced across their jewel-toned surfaces. Small hands, like miniature clock parts, pointed to seemingly random sections, spelling out clues only a trained Naimei could understand. And the steady hum they'd emitted while apart had become a loud purr, occasionally interrupted by a clicking noise as they moved.

In an ideal world, the clicks would stop. Everything would be precisely still and balanced. But the Ways were *never* precisely still and balanced. That, Chloe did remember from her lessons. They were finicky things; immensely confusing and vague. Each section represented a different *something*. Some indicated places; some indicated people; some indicated the barrier between the dead and the living.

To find the imbalance, the Naimei had to recalibrate them, and then work to see what changed. The process was tedious at best and laborious at worst. The only sure sign of progress was the degree of skewed angles; the closer the

Ways physically were to an imbalance, the further out of line they'd become.

Lather, rinse, repeat.

It was never-ending and convoluted. There were never direct answers; never solid foundations. Just clues.

Always more clues, Chloe thought, staring at the instruments sitting on her knobby kitchen table. They contorted at such impossible angles she had to bite back the urge to reach out and steady them.

"Wow," Chloe whispered, looking up at her cousin. He stood, leaning over the table, his weight braced on his hands. "I haven't seen them like this since . . . since . . ."

"The Vanishing," Alex finished, eyeing the silver contraption with barely suppressed astonishment.

Chloe had been young then. But she still remembered the Ways sitting on a kitchen table in one of her family's homes, her parents hunched and whispering over them.

"Is this . . . Does that mean . . . ?" she asked quietly, a note of panic in her voice. The Naimei didn't perish from the human enemy of age. But they still had to leave the world sometime—not that it made it any nicer when that time came.

Especially for those abandoning families. Children.

Me, Chloe thought.

No one knew where the Naimei went after the Vanishing. Another world, another existence, maybe. They were certainly never heard from again.

"Did you study *at all?*" Alex said icily, pulling her out of her thoughts. He gestured toward the instruments on the table. "Did you even look at what they're showing you?"

She scowled. Inside, she breathed a sigh of relief. The Vanishing was *not* something she was prepared to deal with. Cautiously, she gazed at the gleaming silver tools.

It had been a long time since she'd last tried to read them. During a lull in her hunting, to be exact. She'd constructed them, haphazardly, on this very table, hoping they would lead her to a more interesting quarry, a more compelling fight. There'd been a slight lilt to one of the sectored domes, but halfway through the initial calculations, she'd given up and marched into the city. She did find a fight that night, but it was thanks to the inebriated girl who'd made an easy target of herself in a dark alley, not the Ways.

This time, she tried harder to focus, to recall Mikhail's attempts at teaching her the coded language. The Ways were read from right to left. She moved her gaze to the right end of the table and frowned at the red orb with a solid gold line down the middle. The small indicator hand pointed to the left of the line.

"Come on!" Alex snapped. "Honestly, Chloe, the start is the easiest part."

She glared up at him. "If I'm wasting your time, why don't you just tell me what it all means?"

He threw his hands up in frustration. "Then how will you ever learn?"

"If this isn't the Vanishing, I should have plenty of time," she said through gritted teeth.

A sigh fell from his lips. "Fine. Okay. That line, the one you were trying so desperately to figure out is—"

"The Line of Styx," Chloe interrupted, memory blooming. "The line between the living and the dead."

Alex nodded. "Yes. The left side is the dead. You see the scales running from zero to nine?" He gestured to small engravings etched around the orb. The indicator was pointing to VIII. "That's the length of time the problem has been gone from the living."

"So . . ." Chloe mumbled, trying to grasp at a potential explanation. Her immediate thought was a spirit, but that couldn't be true.

Spirits barely had enough energy to manifest themselves, much less throw the world out of balance.

Her cousin stayed silent, drumming his fingers gently on the table while he waited for her to put the pieces together on her own. When she didn't offer anything else, he rolled his eyes and continued, pointing to a sliding scale intricately carved with runes. "This describes the force, magic, or elements that might be in use . . . and this," he gestured to a sphere almost all the way on the left, "is the Continuum."

The Continuum. Chloe was familiar with that, as well. It indicated race. On the right side, the Naimei. Then witches, elementals, and everything in between, reaching humans on the far side of the sphere. Humans bled into shifters, weres, vampires, and then, so far around the circle that they ended up next to the Naimei were:

"Demons," Chloe said softly. The hand was pointing right at them.

As she watched, it waved counter-clockwise ever so slowly, hovering somewhere between human and witch before moving back, pausing slightly as it crossed vampire, and finally returning to demon.

"Chloe," Alex said, sliding into the seat across from her. He looked pale. Tired. Serious. "Are you familiar with Pan and Damonos?"

"Sure," Chloe said, surprised. "They're the forces of chaos, right? The reason dark supernaturals exist." She gestured to the names on that side of the Continuum: shape-shifters, weres, vampires. "The opposite of the Naimei. The reason why we're here to create balance in the first place. It's a bedtime story."

"Not just a bedtime story." Alex's voice was hard. Heavy.

Her first reaction was to laugh, but looking into her cousin's eyes—the cold blue of a winter morning—she stopped. "What do you mean?"

"Pan and Damonos are more than just a force. They're . . . well, they existed. Breathing, walking, demons. The Originals. They were banished from this world, like the stories say; they've been banished for a long time." He paused. "But we think . . . the Ways point to . . . well."

She chewed her lip as he sucked in a deep breath.

"Chloe, we think someone is trying to bring them back."

"You . . . you're sure . . . ?" She felt cold. The stories always featured destruction before victory. If they were true . . .

He shook his head slowly from side to side, as if trying to empty it. "Clearly, something—someone—has been at work, staying under the radar of the Ways. Keeping out of sight. They've no doubt unearthed something that has led to this, but you saw the needle. It's not just one person."

"Where is this happening?"

Their gazes fell on the last orb in the cycle, a vivid blue one. Proximity.

"When I looked at the Ways this morning, that orb was skewed due North," Alex said quietly.

It was now standing poised at attention, no tilt in any direction whatsoever.

"It's happening here. In Molton," Chloe said, excitement rising in her voice. She stood quickly, her chair squeaking against the hardwood. There was only one reason her cousin would share this with her. "I get to help! You came here because you want my help with the fight!"

Alex suppressed a laugh. "Nice try, Cousin."

Chloe's face fell. "What?"

"I came here to tell you what's happening. To give you a heads up. Ask you to keep your ears open; listen for information, for leads. And to, for the love of God, stop your pointless hunting! Apparently life and common sense finally beat me to that punch though." He stared pointedly at her casted arm. "If we're lucky, we'll finish this thing before it begins. There will be no fight. Which is why all *you* need to do is learn the Ways, monitor them, and keep track of your city."

Chloe opened her mouth to argue, but Alex was already turning away, stalking toward a bookcase. He lifted a thick volume from the bottom shelf; it was dustier than the Ways themselves had been.

"You've neglected your studies. Pick them up again." He dropped the book. It landed with a heavy *thump* next to the Ways, but despite the impact, the silver instruments barely wavered. "If you're lucky, we'll let you help find the human."

With that, he turned and walked out the door. Chloe followed him to the stoop, but it was no use; as soon as he crossed the threshold, his form contracted in on itself and disappeared.

THREE

After cursing Alex's name for a good hour, Chloe sat down on the overstuffed couch in the living room, trying desperately to rationalize her feelings. If the current imbalance could be righted without a fight . . . well, maybe that was a good thing. If the villains of her childhood fairy tales stayed where they were, things would be better. Not as exciting, but better.

Being assigned to learn the Ways, though. She pulled a face at the very thought. At least it would be something to do, now that her vampire hunting days were over.

She stared down at her arm, the voice of the vampire who'd attacked her echoing in her thoughts.

"Why? She was going to die anyway! This was her only chance and . . . and you . . . you . . . I loved her!"

She shook her head firmly. *No time for that now.*

She shuffled over to the table, brushing the remaining layer of dust off the leather-bound tome Alex had dropped there. The book once belonged to her parents, and their parents, and their parents' parents, and countless generations hundreds of years before that.

Begrudgingly, she picked it up. Cradling it in her arms, she returned to the now bright living room and burrowed into a particularly worn corner of the couch. She opened the book, letting the yellowed pages fall limply as they saw fit.

The drone of monotonous, outdated writing buzzed through her head, allowing the night's exertions to catch up with her. Her eyes drooped as she slid another page over without seeing what was on it. After five more, the warmth of the mid-morning sun pulled her into sleep.

❧

"Mikhail?" she breathed into the gloom. It was raining outside. Storming, pouring. Every so often, lightning lit up the sky, but the thunder never came.

Her brother was standing at the window, his back to her. He already looked different. Normally, he stood with a sort of careless slouch. But not now. His back was stick straight; his hands clutching at the windowsill. The scars and tattoos wrapped around his muscled arms seemed to pop with tension.

He was dripping wet. His hair—his shaggy, brown hair—was plastered to his skull. His shirt and pants were dark from the rain, as if he had run out in it suddenly, and a puddle of water was forming at his bare feet.

"Mikhail!" she said more desperately.

Something was wrong; something had to be wrong. The way her parents had been whispering over the silver instruments she was not yet able to touch. The way her mother's face had looked as she put her back to bed, tucking her in with her favorite quilted blanket—the blanket she still held as she ran into the room.

Her brother turned to face her, tears mingling with the rainwater on his face. She tripped on the fabric's corner, sprawling onto the ground.

Everything was all wrong.

❧

Chloe sat bolt upright on the couch.

"Ugh," she sighed, swinging her legs to the ground and cradling her head in her hands.

The book was lying on the floor, blessedly closed. Although the pages had been sealed long ago with several Naimei spells, she dreaded the lecture she would get if Alex saw she had somehow managed to crumple or damage them. Especially if it was because she'd fallen asleep while reading.

Slowly, she sucked in a deep, calming breath. Her heart felt like it was going a million miles an hour, as if she were still that scared little girl tripping over her blanket. She glanced at the window. The sun that had been streaming in when she fell asleep had all but vanished; the soft colors of twilight twinkled through the blinds.

That wasn't surprising. Even if vampires were not strictly creatures of the night, they were certainly more active once the sun set. As were the people hunting them.

But even with her old schedule and patterns behind her, the night didn't help slow her heartbeat. It made her restless, agitated; there was no way she'd get more studying done. She would have to go out, even if not to hunt. There were still things she was after in the darkness.

Her previous night in the woods hadn't yielded what she expected. Not that she knew what, exactly, she'd been expecting. Ever since her last fight, she'd had the distinct impression she was being followed. It wasn't much; a flash of a familiar figure, the retreating back of someone she was sure she'd seen before. Never enough to prove anything other than a potential penchant for paranoia, but she was certain. She knew what she saw.

Curiosity swirled in her thoughts as she plucked at a stray bandage on her arm.

Why was she being followed? Had they seen the fight? Was it related to that? They probably thought she was a strong witch. So few knew the Naimei by name anymore.

She had to know what they wanted.

In a matter of minutes, she'd changed into a fresh outfit—this one including a dark leather jacket with an extra knife up the sleeve—and left her house, crossing the yard toward the parkway.

Her heart trilled under the adrenaline that came with hunting; her knives had a pleasant weight to them. Vampires were often too quick for guns, and there was always a chance Naimei magic would interfere with even the simplest of firing mechanisms. Knives, she never had to worry about. Especially when she could move as fast as her prey.

They're not my prey anymore, she forced herself to remember. *You're not hunting. You're just . . . searching.*

She trekked along the edge of the park near a string of small cafés. Her plan had been to sit in the open until her secret friend made an appearance, and then follow them. Turn the tables.

There was no way she could do that now, though; not with the electric hum of energy coursing through her veins. She would have to settle for food and a stroll through the park. There was no reason, if she was being followed, that her stalker wouldn't show up there, as well.

The server at Café Corazon tried desperately to catch her eye as he handed her the wrapped Panini she'd ordered. He was handsome, to be sure, with chiseled features that screamed there was an aspiring actor resumé with his name on it somewhere. A romantic foray with a human was not a weapon she was prepared to arm her cousin with, though, so she smiled politely and ducked her head as she left the restaurant.

She headed to the far side of the park, intending to meander its paths back toward home. That should give her secret friend, if indeed she had one, enough time to show up. The closer to home the confrontation occurred, the better; if it didn't go her way, she could always get back to safety. And if it did . . . well, it spared her a long walk once her purpose was served.

She kept her pace slow as she chewed the sandwich, strolling from path to path. Every now and again she would change directions, looping back and around. She tried as hard as possible to make it look spontaneous, but she was desperate for a glimpse of the figure she'd been seeing for days.

There weren't a lot of people in the park; the sun had gone down, and it was a weeknight. Only the warm, comfortable weather kept a few pedestrians out, and they weren't lingering. She imagined most were on after-dinner strolls, or using the park as a more pleasant thoroughfare for foot traffic. Soon, it would be late enough she'd be guaranteed to be alone.

The flash came after the next corner. It was quick; she wasn't even sure she'd seen it. Down toward the street, a familiar looking back, wrapped in a dark jacket not unlike her own, had dodged behind a tree as a couple exited the park.

Perfect, she thought. She was about to dash over and demand answers when a sound came, very quietly, from behind her.

"Hello," said a soft, male voice.

Despite all her training, she jumped. *Relax, Chloe,* she scolded. *It's not the same person. You were watching. Even the fastest vampires can't move that quickly.*

Slowly, she turned to face the person who had spoken. He was definitely not the one she'd seen dodge behind the tree. There was no dark jacket—just a simple t-shirt over denim. His stature was all wrong, too; medium height, slim build. The brief glimpses she'd seen of her potential stalker, even at a distance, told her he was taller.

There was something different about this boy, though. His movements. His stance.

Vampire.

"Sorry, I didn't mean to startle you," he said with a slight, encouraging smile, "I just saw that you've been walking around the park for awhile. Are you new in town? Did you get lost in here?"

Chloe didn't respond, scanning him again instead. He had a shock of shaggy dark hair and the painfully dark eyes of a vampire. It looked like, at some point, he might have had blue eyes, but time and blood had reduced them to near black. His face was young; it was impossible to place an age. Late teens? Early twenties? Younger, older?

Eighteen, she decided. This boy was probably changed sometime around eighteen. He didn't seem to be especially old, by vampire standards; not new, but definitely not old. Certainly not skilled enough to realize who or what he was currently talking to.

She looked back toward the place she'd seen the figure disappear, unconcerned about taking her eyes off the young vampire. He was clearly looking for an easy, cooperative meal; there would be no surprise attack. She squinted into the darkened tree line, but could see no trace of anyone, hidden or otherwise.

"All that's over that way is a bunch of old cafés. They're closed by now, though," the boy said, cocking his head to one side. "Were you looking for a place to get a bite?"

Chloe sighed. Why did vampires always incorporate puns into their conversation? Did they try, or did it just happen? She turned back to face him. Despite the intentions she knew he had, his face looked earnestly helpful. She wondered if, in addition to feeling real, human emotions, vampires were capable of conversations that didn't house ulterior motives? Maybe this was the perfect opportunity to put her new rules into resolve.

No hunting. Time to see vampires as something other than prey.

"Listen, Vampire," she said, forcing herself to keep a level voice. There was no need for open hostility; no need to blame her lost search on the mostly innocent. "I'm not lost. And I'm certainly not about to be your nightly meal."

The effect of her words was more or less what she'd expected, confirming her suspicions; he'd thought he was talking to an oblivious human woman. He jumped back, lowering into a fighting stance as he surveyed her from head to toe.

"You're the hunter they've been talking about," he snarled, his fangs extended.

Despite the signs of imminent violence, Chloe didn't move. In fact, her only reaction was to arch an eyebrow. She was being talked about? That was news.

"What's being said about me?"

His dark eyes skimmed over her again. "That you're deadly. And . . . and beautiful," he muttered, his voice dropping to a near growl.

Well. That would be flattering if it hadn't come from someone who looked ready to kill me, she thought. She held her hands up in a placating gesture. "Hey, look, I don't do that anymore. I'm, uh . . ." she considered confessing she was in the middle of a moral dilemma, but found it more prudent to finish with, ". . . retired. From hunting."

"Liar!" the vampire snarled, his hands clamped into fists. At least he wasn't reaching for her obvious weakness—the casted arm not quite hidden by the leather of her jacket.

"Look," she said, trying to keep the exasperation out of her voice. *You're done hunting, you're done hunting . . .* "I'm not out to hurt you, okay? I was just looking for someone. You came up to me, remember? I'm sorry if I killed any of your friends, or—"

"The vampires you killed were lowlifes," he spit, narrowing his eyes at her. "They're not missed."

"Well, good," she mused. He was starting to sound a bit like her cousin, though she doubted Alex would appreciate the irony of that comparison. "I'm not out to make any more vampire enemies." *Lord knows I have enough of those already.*

The boy let out a forced laugh. "So, what? You're trying to make some vampire friends?"

"No! I . . ." Alex's words crept back into her head: *Keep your ears open; listen for information, for leads.* "Well . . . maybe," she said, an apologetic note of confusion tinting her otherwise steady voice.

It seemed to confuse the vampire in front of her, too. His position relaxed, just a little. "What?"

"I'm sorry," Chloe said, taking a deep breath. "Look, it's been a long day. I'm just looking . . . well. Let's start over. My name's Chloe." She stretched out her hand, the undamaged right one.

The vampire bared his fangs at her. She could understand the sentiment; the simple gesture made her spine stiffen and her skin crawl.

"Hey, whoa. Okay." She retracted her hand and reached slowly to her side, removing the knife from its sheath—the boy let out a low growl—and dropping it to the dirt. "There. Happy?" She didn't touch the knife hidden in her sleeve. She wasn't stupid.

For a moment, he simply stared at the blade. Then his stance straightened to something less aggressive, something more . . . well, social.

"I'm Sam." He didn't offer a hand, and his gaze still looked wary.

"Sam," she repeated, "It's nice to meet you."

He let out an unconvinced grunt in response, but after a moment, he, too, spoke. "Why are you out at night if you aren't hunting?"

She bit her lip. Was there any harm in telling him? Probably not—he was too young to know anything, anyway. "I thought someone was following me. I was trying to lure them out."

Sam tilted his head to the side again. A trademark expression of curiosity? "And did you find them?"

"I thought I might have. Before you interrupted," she added dryly.

"Sorry," he said, without sounding like he meant it.

She shifted her weight uncomfortably. She wasn't sure what to say during a conversation with a vampire. "You wouldn't know anything about that, would you? Notice anyone funny around?"

"Funny?" He shrugged, crossing his arms over his chest. "If you mean other vampires, sure. There are a lot of us in town. But . . ." He looked away. "But if anyone else was following you, they were hiding it well."

So. He'd been following her, too. Or at least watching. "Uh . . . well. Thanks. I guess. Have you noticed, uh, anything else? Around town?" She cringed at the awkward phrasing.

It was his turn to raise an eyebrow. "Even if I had, why would I tell you?"

"What's in it for me," in other words, she thought, frowning. She contemplated pointing out the fact she hadn't tried to kill him yet, but that might shatter the rocky foundation they'd just established.

Foundation of what? she wondered vaguely. *Friendship? Is this how friendships with vampires start?*

She was just about to ask him that very question, to find out if trading favors was somehow customary, when another voice spoke instead.

"Chloe!"

She grimaced. *Alex*. She could feel him approaching, walking up the path behind her. Sam looked curiously over her shoulder.

"Damn it, Chloe, I told you to stop hunting," Alex said sharply as he drew level with her.

All curiosity vanished from Sam's face. He released one last growl in Chloe's direction, eyes narrowed, before turning on his heel and running at top speed from the forest.

"Sam!" Chloe called hopelessly. There went her potential vampire friend, her potential lead. "Thanks a lot, Alex. I was just trying to—"

"Save it," he said, reaching out to grab her arm. Her left arm. Chloe winced, but she barely even had time to do that before he pulled them both through space. In an instant, they vanished from the park and reappeared in front of her house.

Chloe let out a pained gasp and staggered forward. The Naimei method of travel was not agonizing by any means—it was tiring for the person enacting it, but it wasn't painful. Unless you were pulled into nothingness and back by a grievous injury, of course.

"Gah!" she exclaimed, shouldering her way through the front door. She whirled to face her cousin. "You could've given me some warning, Alex. You made me leave my favorite knife behind."

Just as he had earlier, he waved her comments away as inconsequential. "You'll get a new favorite. There are more important things going on. I've been looking for you for hours. Why," his eyes narrowed, "were you not studying the Ways as instructed?"

Chloe scowled. She plopped into a chair at the kitchen table and held her right hand over her left arm; basic pain relief was one skill she hadn't ignored. "I *was* studying them. And then I wasn't."

"And then you were out playing vampire hunter again," he corrected.

"I wasn't hunting!" She shouted before pausing to suck in a steadying breath. "I was doing the other half of what you told me to."

Alex crossed his arms, leaning back against the door frame and fixing her with a skeptical look. "I don't remember telling you to do anything else."

She took a moment to frown at her arm, and then, content it was still in one piece, looked up at her cousin. "'Keep your ears open,' remember? I was looking for potential, uh, informants."

He snorted with derision. "A naïve young vampire? God, Chloe, just because you don't want to kill them anymore doesn't mean you have to buddy up to them. They're not known for their kindness or honesty."

"You and Mikhail both have vampire friends."

"No," Alex said pointedly, "we both know vampires who happen to know a lot of supernatural news. We exchange information; we don't stand around chatting at all hours."

"Sam wasn't vicious. And I was just getting somewhere when you showed up," Chloe answered defensively. It was a lie, but she didn't want Alex to be right about this, too.

If he doubted her, he didn't say so. Instead, he waved his hand again, discounting her argument as frivolous. "Never mind that. I came back to tell you something important: we found one of them."

Instantly, Chloe's ears perked up. Maybe her chance at a dangerous adventure wasn't dead after all. "Which? The vampire? The demons?"

"The human," Alex responded.

Chloe's face fell.

"Rus has been pouring over the Ways, consulting every book of genetic lines . . . he suspects some latent psychic abilities, but it's still unclear how she might be connected. You know," he said seriously, "This should be a lesson to you. The Ways can yield quick results if you're dedicated to quality research and—"

"Why are you telling me this?" she cut in.

"Because," he said slowly, frustration creeping into his voice, "all signs point to her being here. And we want you to find her."

Chloe bit her lip. She should have been glad to be included. But finding a human? Where was the excitement? The danger? The difficulty? "Find her, fine. Then what?"

Alex shrugged. "Watch her. Talk to her. Befriend her, I don't know. Figure out what she knows, what she is—does she actually have powers? Does she realize what she can do? Figure out her importance and any immediate danger. Decide if she's worth our time, or if she can, at least, lead us to someone who is."

Chloe sighed. *Decide if she's worth our time.* They want to know if she's the one human aware of something diabolic unfolding? Okay. No problem.

"Who knows," Alex continued, "Maybe she's the mastermind behind this whole thing."

She knew he was saying it for her benefit, but it didn't make her feel any better about being handed the busywork. "How am I supposed to find her?"

For one horrifying moment, she was afraid he was going to direct her back to the Ways. His smile certainly made it seem like a strong possibility. But then he reached into his back pocket, extracted a stack of papers, and passed them to her.

"*That* is how you'll find her."

Skeptically, she accepted the papers, unfolding the top one carefully. The first line read, in bold script:

MOLTON AREA HIGH SCHOOL

"She's a high school student?" Chloe asked, scanning over the page, which also contained words like "Grade Twelve" and "Fall Schedule". Who on earth was seeking a high school student for their evil plots?

"She is . . ." Alex said carefully, watching her over the top of the paper. His tone reeked of a hanging "and" statement that was yet to come.

Chloe frowned at him. Was she missing something? The girl was a student; find her after class. No big deal. She scanned the page again, searching for a name, some indication of who she was looking for.

But the human girl's name wasn't on the paper. The only name on it, in the same bold print, read proudly:

CHLOE MORAINE

"No way," she said quietly. Then, more loudly, "No way! No, Alex! You did *not* enroll me in a human *high school!*"

"You're right, I didn't. Rus did," he laughed. But at Chloe's glowering expression, he held his hands up defensively. "Chloe, please, be realistic. How else are you supposed to get close to this girl?"

"God, I don't know . . . anywhere else but high school, maybe? Why can't one of you go?" She slapped the schedule down on the table next to the still happily purring, woefully lopsided Ways.

"You're the youngest, Chloe. You stopped aging the earliest."
He crossed the room. Selecting the seat across from her, he began
disassembling the silver tools.

As much as she wanted to argue, he had a point. If she
could pass as late teens to early twenties, he would be at least
five years older than anything she pretended to be. Finally, she
mumbled, "Mikhail stopped young, too."

"Chloe," he said, fixing her with a serious stare. "Honestly.
Mikhail? Have you looked at his arms lately?"

An image of her brother's twisting, twining tattoos filled her
mind. "He could hide them if he wanted to."

Alex sighed. "You know how much effort that would take,
hiding his appearance from a school full of students and
teachers. Plus, some of those marks were made by decidedly
non-human talent. They would be next to impossible to hide."

"So it has to be me."

"It has to be you," he repeated. A smirk tugged at the
corner of his lips. "I thought you wanted this. Adventure. Danger."

"There's no adventure or danger in high school," Chloe said
coldly.

"How would you know?" Alex retorted. "You've never been."

Naimei didn't typically attend human institutions, but that
didn't mean they were unfamiliar with the culture of them. "I
know enough," she said stubbornly.

"Then go to school, young lady." He was clearly enjoying
himself. "Oh, I almost forgot . . . here, take this. Mikhail left it
with me; it was your parents'. Might help you find what you're
looking for."

Alex extracted a small, carved box, not unlike the one that held
the Ways, from his pocket. Chloe grudgingly accepted it and flipped
open the lid. Inside was a green orb with a long, gold hand in the
middle. It might have looked like a compass, if it had any markings;
instead, the entire thing was blank.

"Thanks," Chloe muttered. She recognized the device immediately. It was a Finder, a compressed version of the Ways. Using it was significantly less annoying, but, she had to admit, it was also significantly less accurate.

"Classes start tomorrow!" Alex twittered as he crossed to the door, leaving Chloe without a backwards glance.

She groaned, looking up at the clock above the doorway. It proudly proclaimed that it was already two o'clock in the morning.

Homeroom would start in six hours.

FOUR

The digital clock mounted to the wall glared an angry 7:47 a.m.; Chloe, blue eyes narrowed, glared right back. As if sensing her stare, or at least her presence, the red numbers gave a shudder, blinked twice, and dimmed to almost black.

Technology was no friend of the Naimei.

At the moment, she rather enjoyed that fact, taking pride in the ailing electronic. 7:47 a.m. was a ghastly time to be standing at a locker. *Her* locker. The entire thing, from stopping in the office for her official schedule to receiving a stack of borrowed textbooks, was horribly embarrassing.

She had no business pretending to be a human high school senior. Despite what she'd told Alex, she knew nothing of high school beyond the basic conventions, structure, and potential for heaping amounts of teenage angst.

And yet, here she was.

She stifled a yawn as she sifted through the books, selecting the ones she'd need for her first few hours. This schedule was the exact opposite of the nocturnal one she'd been keeping for months. Waking up with the early morning sun felt unnatural, wrong.

But maybe that was how high school was supposed to feel.

She tried to kill as much time at her locker as possible, plucking out a blank notebook and a handful of pens, labeling a folder. The second semester was already underway, and the students around her were in no rush to continue their classes. It wasn't the first day. They didn't need to be early; there was no one to impress.

Once the crowd of kids talking beside lockers and classrooms began to thin, Chloe picked her way down the corridors to her assigned homeroom, the Finder Alex had given her clutched in one hand.

She paused in the doorway of Room 212, evaluating who'd already arrived. Despite the fact it was only five minutes to the bell, there were few occupants.

Two bespectacled kids sat at the front of the room, every textbook they'd ever owned piled on top of their desks. Sitting nearest to the door was a twitchy boy, glancing from the clock to the hallway, already ready for it to be over. Another group of boys sat in the back, laughing loudly over something drawn in a notebook. A petite girl with tawny, brown hair occupied the very center of the room, doodling with a purple pen, head bent over her work. And behind her, two girls—one with tight blonde curls spilling down half her back, the other with a red pixie cut—had their heads together in conspiratorial whispers. Every now and again, the red-haired one would release a malicious laugh at something the blonde said.

God, Chloe thought, *I hope it's not one of them.* She shook her head slowly and sighed. She'd lingered in the doorway long enough already, but she had one more thing to do. As inconspicuously as possible, she flipped open the Finder. This lot hardly looked like anyone special—she half expected it to spin around, facing somewhere else in the school. But the needle quivered once and pointed to the girl drawing in her notebook.

At that moment, the redhead let out a particularly cutting trill of laughter. Drawing Girl looked briefly over her shoulder and then returned to her notebook with a quick eyeroll.

Well, Chloe mused, *at least she has good taste.*

She crossed the room and slid into an empty desk next to Drawing Girl. Several kids slipped in behind her as the clock ticked to 7:57. She made a show of examining her schedule, placing her books noisily in front of her.

Drawing Girl looked up, curious. She had a kind face; smooth, pale skin with rosy cheeks; wide set eyes in a deep gray color, so neutral they almost seemed to absorb the colors around her. When she spoke, her lips turned up in a smile. "Oh. Are you new?"

Chloe tried to put a pleasant expression on her face. Time to act the part. "Yes! Yes, I am."

"Cool," Drawing Girl said, her small smile spreading into a grin. "Molton's nice. You'll like it here. I'm Aurelia, by the way."

"Chloe," she returned.

"It's very nice to meet you. Where were you from? Before you came here, I mean."

Chloe offered up a shrug. "Homeschooled." It wasn't a lie that would make her popular, perhaps, but it was plausible; and it spared her from creating any elaborate scenarios.

"*Home*schooled?" said a shrill voice from behind. It was the blonde girl; apparently, her ears perked up at the presence of a newcomer.

"I'm pretty sure that's what I said, yeah," Chloe replied coolly, fixing the girl with a firm stare.

The blonde rolled her eyes, giving her hair a toss before returning her attention to Chloe. She might have been pretty, if she didn't have a perpetual scowl in place. It heightened the appearance of her sharp features, making them look pinched and sour as she gave Chloe an appraising once-over.

"Well," she answered haughtily, "I guess that explains the outfit." She turned to face her cohort as the redhead snorted into her folder.

Aurelia shook her head, muttering something along the lines of, "Whatever, Corrine," before looking up at Chloe with a slightly forced smile. "What does your schedule look like?"

Obligingly, Chloe passed her the piece of paper and tried to act surprised as Aurelia beamed, exclaiming: "We have all the same classes!"

She was graciously accepting Aurelia's offer to act as guide—trying to assure her what a help that would be, falsely claiming an ability to get lost almost anywhere—when Mrs. Patten walked in, followed closely by the bell and the last of her homeroom class.

Mrs. Patten was more or less what Chloe had expected based on her class's attendance habits. She was soft-spoken, and probably a pushover, but otherwise seemed like a fairly intelligent woman trapped in the wrong occupation.

Taking her class schedule back from her new best friend, Chloe skimmed it again and came away slightly disappointed that she would be forced to sit through another whole class with the woman—no doubt watching as her students took advantage of her—in the hours after lunch.

When the bell rang for first period (a halfhearted *brrrinngg* due to Chloe's presence), she tried to look as inefficient as possible. She slowly gathered her things, making sure to knock at least one book to the floor.

She heard the blonde exclaiming to her friends on the way out: "Can you believe it? *Home*schooled!" But Aurelia, who was patiently waiting to show Chloe to her next class, ignored it. Chloe followed her lead.

For the next few hours, she continued to act perplexed as she gazed around the hallways, haltingly repeating directions

Aurelia rattled off. She nodded and smiled obediently at the girl's stories, at the people she pointed out. The act of high school was more exhausting than high school itself.

If I wasn't expected to be her friend, this would be much easier, Chloe thought. Keeping a silent and distant watch wouldn't teach her as much about her target, though, assuming there was anything to be learned. Aurelia was sweet, but showed no signs of extraordinary powers, and it wouldn't be the first time the Ways were befuddled in the midst of a large unbalancing.

Regardless, Chloe kept watching. She waited for something to happen all through Trigonometry, American History, French, and Study Hall. But nothing did.

As they headed down the long hall to the gym, Chloe was certain something would finally emerge. Today's Physical Education game was dodgeball, the perfect sport to trigger supernatural abilities. But it quickly became apparent that Aurelia wasn't prone to precognition or any other physical manifestation of power. She was immediately pummeled by the flying foam spheres.

Chloe mimicked Aurelia's level of athleticism, allowing a particularly vicious blond boy built like a tree trunk to hit her so she could sit.

The girl offered her a sporting high five for staying in the game so long, and then nodded to her casted arm. "I'm surprised you played with that. Most kids use injuries as an excuse to sit out."

"Oh. They do? Uh . . . well. High pain tolerance, I guess." Chloe shrugged, trying to cover up the flaw in her average-teenager cover. "And I just live for dodgeball, since I'm so good at it and all."

The other girl chuckled appreciatively at the self-deprecation. "What did you do to your arm, anyway?"

"Lost a fight," Chloe said vaguely, offering the same half-truth she'd provided her family. It wasn't until the last syllable fell out that she realized it might not be an appropriate reason for a high school senior to be in a cast. But when she looked to Aurelia, the girl was laughing.

"Wow. A fight, huh? Way to be creative about your injuries. I sprained my ankle last year and told the truth about slipping on ice. Didn't do anything for my reputation." She offered a small smile.

Despite Chloe's suspicion that the girl was not at all special, she returned the smile as genuinely as she could.

≈

"Hey! Where are you going?" Aurelia called.

Chloe had just finished stuffing books into her locker and taken off with a much lighter load toward the cafeteria. At Aurelia's call, she stopped.

"Uh . . . to lunch? That's what my schedule says, anyway."

Aurelia chuckled. "Oh, I forgot . . . you wouldn't know. Seniors get senior privilege—we can eat off campus if we want."

"Oh," Chloe offered as a response. Where they ate didn't matter much to her. She'd been looking forward to seeing her new friend interact with other people in hopes of eliciting some new behavior. "Don't you have friends you need to meet up with, or something?"

The other girl cast her gray eyes downward. "Well, uh . . . not really. I mean, the people I usually eat with . . . I'm not super close with them or anything. They won't miss me."

Finally, *that* was something Chloe could use; often, humans would distance themselves subconsciously from things they sensed to be different. Aurelia was on friendly terms with everyone, but no one seemed to make an effort to be her friend? Certainly seemed to point at the possibility she was supernatural. "Oh. Well, yeah. Sure. Let's go get lunch, then." Chloe offered a smile to try and cover Aurelia's embarrassment.

After a brief stop at her own locker, Aurelia led Chloe to the side entrance of the building. Molton Area High School was set in the northernmost district that could still be considered part of the city. Two sides bled quickly into suburbia. The others were urban enough to offer immediate views of offices and apartment buildings, as well as several small eateries not far away.

"Oh—hold on," Aurelia said, pausing in the doorway. "I think I forgot my wallet . . . wait . . ." She paced back a few steps, pawing through her bag with one hand.

Chloe leaned back against a darkened classroom door but straightened almost immediately as the hall rang with the unmistakable sound of something being thrown into a row of lockers.

At the far end of the hall, where it branched to another part of the school, the gawky kid who'd won during dodgeball was sprawled on the ground, his expression pained. The burly, blond boy he'd knocked out of the game stood above him, a nasty snarl plastered on his face.

"You made me look really stupid back there, Roger. How are athletics supposed to be *my thing* if I'm seen losing to a scrawny little nerd like you?"

"I—I I was j-j-just trying to play th-the game . . ." squealed Roger.

The big blonde scooped him up by the front of his shirt, slamming him into the lockers again and holding him there with one hand. "The only game you need to be playing is Stay On My Good Side." He pulled his fist back for a punch.

"Hey!" Chloe shouted, taking a few quick steps forward.

"Chloe, don't!" Aurelia tried to make a grab for her arm, but Chloe stepped out of reach.

The blond boy turned to face her. His fist relaxed ever so slightly. "Who the hell are you?"

Before she could reply, a girl's sneering voice cut in: "Well, if it isn't Homeschooled, learning all about the big, bad, public school system." The curly-haired blonde from homeroom, the one Aurelia had called Corinne, leaned against the opposing bay of lockers, twirling her hair and smacking her gum.

Chloe narrowed her eyes but kept her voice even and level. "My name's Chloe, in case you've forgotten."

"Look who thinks she's a big shot!" Corinne scoffed, closing the distance between them. "Listen, Girly. You need to learn to stay out of things that don't concern you."

"Oh, but this does concern me," Chloe replied, standing her ground, "It concerns me a lot when a kid is getting beat up for winning at dodgeball."

"That's not the only reason," the blonde boy protested gruffly, "He deserves it."

Distracted, he loosened his grip. Panic-stricken Roger seized the opportunity to tear off down the hallway and disappear around the corner.

All attention was on Chloe now. Her hands tensed as she sank into a stance more conducive to fighting.

"Christ, who do you think you are, some superhero vigilante?" Corinne rolled her eyes, shouldering past Chloe hard enough to spill the notebook and papers she'd been holding.

"Come on, Derek," she ordered.

The burly blond gave Chloe a scowl before following.

"Enjoy your last *easy* day of high school," Corinne added over her shoulder.

Chloe waited until she could no longer hear their footsteps before releasing a heavy sigh.

Aurelia, misinterpreting the noise as one of fear and relief rather than frustration, raced forward to offer reassurances and help gather the strewn papers.

"God, Chloe, that was awesome, but really . . . you didn't need to do that."

Chloe just shook her head. "They're nasty pieces of work."

"Well, Corinne's just acting like that because you look like . . . well, you know," Aurelia said, shoving some of the papers into the notebook. At Chloe's quizzical look, she elaborated, "Like you just walked out of a magazine. You know, that's hard for anyone to do in high school."

Chloe shifted uncomfortably at the words. *Note to self,* she thought, *stop brushing hair, start wearing rags to school.* "Whatever. At least she and that guy found each other. They make a good couple."

Aurelia laughed. "They do, but not in the way you're thinking. They're twins," she explained as she passed the papers back to Chloe.

Lost in frustrated thoughts of arrogant human teenagers, Chloe reached out to accept the pile of stuff. As she did, her hand brushed over Aurelia's.

The effect was instantaneous; a sharp shock spread through her entire body. Buzzing filled her ears, like she was on a bad phone connection. She felt a wave of panic even though her heartbeat was steady and her breathing normal. Her eyes locked with Aurelia's, and as she saw the fear hiding in their depths, she realized the panic she felt was not her own.

Chloe tensed in surprise, but even before Aurelia jerked away, the connection was broken.

"Um. So, uh, where do you want to go for lunch?" Aurelia was careful not to meet Chloe's gaze. A red blush was creeping into her cheeks, instantly telling Chloe two things: Aurelia was just as aware of what had happened as she was. And this had happened before.

That tiny bit of proof was all she needed to throw herself back into the job at hand. All the way to the small, kitschy soup shop Aurelia had selected for lunch, Chloe kept up a steady banter, occasionally slipping in probing questions about Aurelia, her family, and her history.

"So, what do your parents do?" she asked as she picked through the last dregs of a salad.

Aurelia paused to swallow a mouthful of soup. "Oh, they're both in some kind of business—buying, selling, litigations, I don't know. They travel a lot. I mean, they didn't used to. It was family first until I hit high school, and then I think they realized I'd need money for college and became super workaholics."

Well, there were no clues there.

She continued the interrogation as innocently as possible for the duration of the meal and the entire walk back to school. By the time they reached the doors, she'd learned that Aurelia had lived in Molton most of her life, she and Corinne had, for a time, been friends in elementary school, and she had a favorite aunt—a school teacher who traveled the world in the summer and never failed to send postcards.

None of it was particularly interesting, and none of it helped to explain Aurelia's ambiguous powers.

The moment the bell rang, the questioning gave way to a long, dry lecture on the next literary classic they'd be embarking on, and Chloe became instantly annoyed at having to continue her investigation in the classroom setting. Though most of the class appeared to be ignoring the teacher, there was no way to talk easily without being noticed; even Aurelia had given up and pulled out her homeroom notebook to resume doodling.

Chloe sighed, opening her own notebook to do the same, but not really following through with the action. Her head felt too full; she was turning over possibilities, potentials, reasons for what had happened and what Aurelia might be. "Latent psychic abilities" was far too broad a title, especially for the unusual burst Chloe had felt. But all of her questioning so far had led to nothing but normal dead ends and more questions.

The final class of the day, Chemistry, offered as little opportunity for conversation as English had. The only real bonus to the subject change was the announcement of a partner project. With a few mumbled words from Chloe, the teacher dazedly pronounced she and Aurelia partners before dividing up the rest of the class and launching into the project instructions.

The long-winded explanation was somewhat meditative to Chloe, who found the drone of their white-haired teacher's voice calming. Embracing the lecture as ambient noise, she stopped fighting the menagerie of conflicting thoughts. Halfway through the period, she reluctantly decided what she needed to do next.

When the bell rang, Chloe's books were already packed away. She stood as Aurelia began tucking her notebook into her bag, and barely paused when the other girl opened her mouth.

"Hey! Chloe! Library? We have to work on this project!"

She turned to face her partner. "Sorry, I have . . . I just have to go. Tomorrow?" She didn't wait to hear Aurelia's response before she took off down the hallway.

She got out of the school quickly, but there were already hordes of students pouring from the doors, making their way to cars parked in the small parking lot, bikes chained at a long rack, or bus stops around the various streets. She didn't bother looking around like she usually did, searching for the flash that had become familiar in the last few weeks.

No, she didn't bother with any of that. For the first time in months, perhaps even years, she knew exactly what—and who—she needed to find.

She discovered a side street not plagued by students and took a quick, final glance around. Slipping between two buildings, she pulled herself into nothingness, and vanished.

FIVE

She reappeared in a quiet alley between two buildings. It had been sunny in Molton, but here, several state lines away, it was overcast, making it seem significantly later than it was. She leaned against one of the alley walls, her heart racing like she'd run from Molton in a full-out sprint. In a way, she had; it took nearly as much effort to use her powers.

After a brief moment, she walked down several blocks to a familiar apartment building. By the time she'd climbed the stairs to the top unit, the sky had released a dull sprinkle.

She tried the doorbell, but when no one answered and the drizzle turned into a downpour, she started knocking in earnest at the peeling, wooden door.

"Alex!" she shouted between pounds. "Alex, open up!"

The door swung open mid-knock, but the man standing behind it was not her dark-haired cousin. He stood taller and his hair was lighter; in the light flooding from the apartment, it took on a slight reddish hue.

"Rus?" Chloe blinked through the thick drops of water that had settled on her lashes.

Rus was her exact opposite in nearly every way. He was tall, she was short. She had dark hair, he had light. He was talented with the Ways—loved them even—and she dreaded the sound of buzzing silver.

But the most significant difference was that he never looked for adventure, never sought a fight. He claimed the aversion came from clumsiness, but Chloe had always suspected he'd had a moral awakening similar to her own. Though his probably had something to do with the balance the Naimei fought to preserve rather than a single race of supernaturals.

"Chloe," he said warmly, stepping back to let her through the door. "I don't think Alex was expecting you. He stepped out to take care of something, but should be back soon."

She ran her non-casted hand over her wet clothes, gently urging her powers forward. With a little effort, the water pulled cleanly from the fibers, forming an undulating orb she lobbed back out onto the stairway. "I wasn't expecting you. Why are you here?"

It was odd to see him anywhere but in his study, pouring over his set of Ways. He hardly ever disassembled them, much less buried them among stacks of ancient tomes. The old books he accumulated never rested; he was constantly sifting through hundreds of years of information and research entrusted to him by his parents before their Vanishing.

He offered her a shrug and indicated a low table in Alex's hodge-podge of living room furniture. There, glinting among items that might have looked at home in a college dorm, was Alex's set of Ways, softly purring just as Chloe's had been. "I came to help Alex channel."

She crinkled her nose. Channeling with other Naimei was incredibly exhausting. She'd only channeled once, when she was very young and trying desperately to help her brother gain a clearer read. She'd spent the next two days in bed, barely able to lift a spoon to feed herself, while Mikhail had slept until midafternoon and then left. He'd returned late that night, proudly declaring he'd eliminated a rogue shape-shifter who'd been about to launch a massive attack on a town of humans.

As she accepted a cushion on the aged, brown couch, she found herself thinking that perhaps it was a good thing she'd found Rus before she'd found Alex. Rus had always been more sympathetic toward her efforts than the rest of the family. And he never bragged. Not that he never had anything to brag about; she just never bothered to follow his academic line of achievement, and he never pushed her to understand it.

"So," he said, seating himself in a recliner next to the couch, "how've you been? I haven't seen you since, well, you know." Rus gestured toward her bandaged arm. "How's it feeling?"

She shrugged. "It's fine, I guess. It hurt a little the other day, but that was just because . . ." *Your brother is an impatient jerk,* she finished.

Rus gave her a knowing smile. "Yeah, Alex said he was in a rush and might have banged you up a bit. He also mentioned you were pretty upset about leaving a knife behind."

Chloe looked down guiltily. Rus had given her the knife when she'd come back from amending an imbalance and proclaimed a fierce desire to start attacking problems at their source. Namely, eliminating vampires before they had a chance to imbalance things.

Alex had rolled his eyes and told her it wasn't their place before launching into a speech about the history of the Naimei.

Mikhail, who'd been in town for a moment, had half-heartedly tried to explain that she was in the wrong and would understand one day. But in the end, just gave her a one-armed hug and left.

Rus had listened to her intently, nodding at all the right moments. When she was done, he hadn't said anything; just stood and left the room. He'd come back with a silver knife—her first true hunting knife—and told her simply to use it wisely.

"Rus," she began, ready to launch into a full apology and

explanation of why her knife had been on the ground in the first place. She hadn't planned on divulging her sudden aversion to vampire hunting; her fear she was being followed; her inkling that, as a species, vampires were not altogether awful. But for Rus, she would admit to all of it.

Before she could get much further, though, he gave her a one-handed wave to indicate she need not elaborate. "It's nothing to worry about, really," he said, then gestured to her bandaged arm. "Let me have a look at that."

She gratefully stretched her injured limb toward him. "Thanks, Rus," she added softly.

He carefully peeled away the layers, eventually removing the thin strips of plastic he'd used to keep the bones in line. From there, he probed her arm gently, feeling for any lingering weaknesses. "How does this feel?"

"Tender," she admitted, "but it doesn't really *hurt*."

"Hm," Rus said, sliding out of his seat and disappearing down the hall. There was a rustling sound from the closet, and then he returned with a cloth and metal brace. He slipped her arm into it and began deftly velcroing. "Humans can be quite ingenious when it comes to healing. Alex picked up this splint last time he injured himself, but it should work just as well for you."

Chloe raised her eyebrows as she inspected the black splint. "When did Alex hurt himself?"

"The last time he lost a fight," Rus said with a sly smile.

Chloe felt the pink heat of a blush creep into her cheeks. Rus knew so many of her secrets, so many of her lies. She should tell him the truth, tell him everything that happened.

"So, what brings you to Alex's doorstep tonight?" he asked.

The words caught in her throat; she'd almost forgotten her original purpose for coming. What she'd been about to say took a 180 degree turn. Instead of explaining the end of her hunting days, she described her first day in high school: the awful injustices endured by human teenagers; finding Aurelia; her disappointment that the girl wasn't anything special, and her amazement when she found out she was.

"You should've felt it, Rus. I've been around psychics, but I've never felt anything like that. It was . . . it was like a phone line. Complete connection. And the craziest thing is, I'm sure it's happened to her before. Even if she doesn't understand it, I know she knows something weird is happening." Chloe shook her head slowly. "God, I just wanted to tell her everything—who I was, why I was looking for her—"

"You *know* that's against the rules, Chloe." She hadn't heard Alex enter, but enter he had. He was already selecting a seat across from her, his hair dripping with rain water. "We don't reveal ourselves unless absolutely necessary."

"But that's unfair. She knows she's different, but she has no idea how! If I could just explain—"

"That's not your job," he said tersely, leaning forward to examine the Ways. His eyes flickered briefly up to her. "But at least you learned something; she has no idea what she is or what she can do, just that she can do something. What else did you find out?"

"Not much," Chloe mumbled, repressing some of the answers she'd gotten out of Aurelia.

"Well, then keep looking. Research. Rus, you have some books that might help, don't you?" Alex said, his gaze sliding over to his brother.

Rus nodded and stood to find the requested tomes.

"Does anyone else have their eye on her?" Alex asked, leaning back into the decrepit couch cushions.

Not on her, no, Chloe thought blandly, thinking of the flash of leather jacket she'd been seeing around town. "Not that I know of."

"Not that you know of? Did you forget to investigate the rest of the school? The area around it?"

"It's a human high school!" Chloe said, throwing her arms up in exasperation.

Alex shook his head, sending drops of water flying about the room. "You know as well as anyone that vampires and every other type of supernatural will try to fit themselves anywhere and everywhere they think they can pass as human. Even high school, remember?"

She cringed. She remembered; it had been one of her last tasks before she'd all but forsaken the Ways for hunting. A young vampire trying to blend into a high school had attended a rugby game, but at the sight of a particularly bloody injury . . . well, the aftermath had not been pretty. "Fine. Okay. But what are you two doing that's so important you're trying to channel?"

Alex fixed her with a cold stare. "Just find out if anyone else wants the girl. Figure out what she can do with those powers. *Then* you can find out what the big kids are working on."

Chloe opened her mouth for an angry retort, but shut it again when Rus entered the room, several large books in his arms.

"For you," he said lightly, handing them off to her. "We won't be gone long; just until we go where we need to go and find what we need to find."

"Ugh!" Chloe said, snapping up the books and storming out the door.

As soon as it clicked shut behind her, she disliked Alex even more. Like so many Naimei dwellings, he'd enacted precautionary enchantments around the perimeter, making it impossible for her to simply vanish off the stoop. She stomped through the rain to the alley she'd appeared in and pulled herself, anger and all, through space.

She appeared on the far side of her small yard. Her house had no such enchantments. It was foolish, perhaps, but convenient; and since her most recent quarries had only been vampires, there was little risk of intrusion from the more magical supernaturals. But she still preferred to aim for the line of trees . . . just in case.

Once again, her heart was racing, though this time she couldn't tell if it was from exertion or anger. For a moment, she stood in the darkened yard with her eyes shut, enjoying a few carefully measured breaths. It was only when she opened them again that she noticed something different.

There, on the doorstep—a small, velvet bag. And glinting out of the top, a familiar wink of silver.

She crossed the yard quickly, dropping the books and drawing her favorite knife from the drawstring sack. A mixture of joy, relief, and confusion flooded through her. Whoever returned it had given it a good polish: the silver of the blade shown in the moonlight. The handle felt solid and steady in her hand, fitting her grip perfectly despite the fact it hadn't been made for her. She sent up a silent thanks.

Who *had* returned it, though? Rus? Definitely not Alex. She frowned.

Another body slammed into her, forcing her face-first into the heavy, wooden door. Years of training were all that kept her from a broken nose; she turned her head just enough that the wood collided, concrete-hard, with her face, the impact knocking the knife from her hand. She cursed as it skittered away and pain burst across her skull.

The vampire grabbed her roughly by the shoulders, spinning her to face him and shoving her against the solid backing of the door. The wind left her lungs as she landed with a painful thud. It took only seconds—the time it took to gasp breath back into her lungs—to recognize the familiar pale, lean form, the dark hair, the bared fangs, before his fingers cinched around her neck.

"S-sam?" she choked, pressing the metal splint into the side of his right wrist, trying to break his grip at its weakest point. *Why couldn't humans decorate their medical supplies with silver?*

"You must think you're pretty clever, Witch," he hissed, his face contorted with rage. It looked so different from the earnest, sincere face she'd seen in the park. "Does pretending to be a retired hunter bag you a lot of bodies?"

Witch. Her first instincts had been correct—he had no idea what she was, what he was dealing with. "I don't know what you're talking about!" she insisted, giving up on the splint and resorting to clawing at his hands in a wasted effort to pull them away from her. Whatever knowledge Sam lacked, he was still incredibly strong.

He let out a low growl and shoved her into the door again, his grip tightening.

Chloe wheezed, "Whatever my cousin said, he didn't know the full story. I wasn't hunting you!" She let go of his wrist with her right hand, dropping her shoulder with a sharp jerk. Sam's eyes instantly darted down to her hand, and his grip relaxed just enough to give her the opening she needed.

She brought her right leg up, sinking her foot into his stomach and kicked. Sam flew backward across the yard, landing with a thump in the grass.

In an instant, he was on his feet again, fangs still bared. "Everyone is nervous. You can't tell me that's not because of you."

"It's not," Chloe rasped, rubbing at the angry red marks he'd left on her throat and only making them redder.

"Liar!" he shouted, rushing at her blindingly fast.

But Chloe was ready. She deftly moved aside, landing a punch, mid-dodge, with her good arm. She heard a satisfying *crack* as his jaw broke. The injury wouldn't last more than a minute—well-fed vampires healed almost instantly—but she could take full advantage of that one injured instant.

His jaw was resetting when she tackled him to the ground, placing one knee firmly on his torso, her knife poised just above his heart. For a moment, she was sure a glimmer of fear reflected in his dark eyes.

"I am not *trying* to hunt you," she said slowly, purposefully.

The fear hardened into firm defiance. "This is how you don't hunt someone?"

Chloe rolled her eyes and cast her knife toward the house. This time, the move was truly dangerous; she didn't have a second blade hidden up her sleeve. *But at least I don't have to worry about losing the knife again.* "Are you ready to believe me yet?"

Sam's eyes narrowed, but he didn't say anything.

"I'm going to let you up now, okay? It'll make things much easier if you don't attack me when I do. Otherwise, we're just going to end up right back here." She held his gaze with her own. "And next time, I won't take it easy on you. Understand?"

Barely, he moved his head up and down.

She stood and took a few steps back.

Sam got up slowly, using none of his supernatural speed. He continued to stare at her, as if unsure what to do next. Chloe crossed her arms, waiting for another accusation, or more likely, for him to turn and run.

"You could start by explaining yourself," she suggested dryly when neither happened. She chose to leave the knife on the ground as a gesture of goodwill, but it was not far off. Just in case.

He kicked angrily at the ground, avoiding her gaze. "I was hunting you before you could hunt me."

"Well, that was obvious," she said with a sigh, stooping to

collect the books that had become strewn across the yard in the struggle. Many of them were leather-bound and hand-written, and she again felt thankful they'd been magically protected years ago; some of them probably wouldn't have survived being roughly dropped to the ground otherwise. "But what about that other part? Everyone is nervous?"

Sam looked off into the distance. "It's nothing."

"It's something," she offered, depositing the books in a tidy pile next to the knife and leaning back on the doorframe. "What did you mean?"

He finally met her gaze. "Something's wrong. And I thought it was you."

Chloe frowned. "Wrong . . . how?"

"People are nervous," Sam repeated with a shrug. "They're . . . well, they're moving."

"If by 'people', you mean vampires, they're always transient," she said gently. "That's not new."

"Shifters aren't," he retorted, looking defensive, "and they've been moving around more than usual, to territories that aren't their own. Everyone's talking about it. Things feel. . . wrong . . . unbalanced."

Chloe snorted before she could reign in her reaction. Sam's expression darkened. "Sorry! Sorry, it's just . . . look, I promise I'm not the one behind unbalancing anything."

"How do I know you're telling the truth?" he demanded.

"I thought we were past this 'untrustworthy' stuff," she said lightly. But when Sam's expression didn't change, she added, "Look, I swear I'm not lying to you, okay? I'm not unbalancing the world. If anything, I'm trying to, uh, fix the situation."

At that, Sam seemed to perk up. "Really? What do you know?"

"Well, uh . . ." Alex's voice seemed to flood her ears: *We don't reveal ourselves unless absolutely necessary.* How much would she be permitted to tell an uninvolved vampire if she couldn't say anything to a semi-involved human? "I'm, uh, dealing more with the human side of things. You know, vampires don't really like me."

"*Humans* are involved?" Sam said, his dark eyes wide. He shook his head quickly though, as if chasing away the thought, and took a step forward. "Whatever. But, you're helping. You could help with the supernatural stuff, too. I mean, you're a witch, right? This whole place smells like witch-magic."

Chloe bit her lip. "I . . . uh. Well. Yeah," she said lamely. She was certainly not a witch, but there was nothing she could say to the contrary. "Look, I have something very specific I have to do. But you could look around. Listen. Find information. If you tell me, I can pass it along to people who are trying to help, too. You know, with the supernatural stuff."

For a moment, she was sure Sam was about to hurl another accusation at her, to refuse to work as her informant unless she gave up more information about her "very specific" assignment. But to her great surprise, he simply cocked his head to the side, and said, "Yeah. Okay."

She held back a sigh of relief. "Good. Well . . . okay then. I guess, just come find me when you have something." She offered a small smile, the first of the exchange. "I'm always around."

Sam nodded. His eyes lingered on her; a long, searching look. He seemed on the edge of saying something, but turned to leave instead. At the very last moment, before he reached the tree line leading back to the city, he turned to face her.

"You're not what I expected," he said. And then, like a shot, he was off, racing through the night.

As Chloe wiped dirt from the shining silver of her knife, she wondered if all her previous encounters with vampires could have ended that easily—and strangely—if she'd simply bargained for their help.

SIX

When Chloe finally made it into her house, ladened with books and the newly returned knife, she deemed it much too late to study. Instead, she dedicated her time to selecting an outfit for the next day—one that wouldn't turn any heads—and pondering the reappearance of her knife.

She'd forgotten to ask Sam if he'd seen who'd placed it, so graciously, on her doorstep. For all she knew, it could have been him—though it seemed unlikely that a vampire would return a knife to a known hunter moments before attacking her. More than likely, it had been one of her cousins. Alex, out of uncharacteristic guilt, maybe, or Rus, out of very characteristic kindness.

Regardless, it won both of them some forgiveness for the exhausting day they'd given her. Trying to fit in at a particularly average high school was harder than expected, and that, on top of actual work—research, the Ways, finding informants—seemed near impossible.

She tried to ignore that thought as she got ready for bed, but it chased her into sleep the moment her head hit the pillow.

❧

When she opened her eyes, she had the distinct sensation she'd spent the entire night running from a mysterious figure in a leather jacket, though she could conjure no memory of the dream beyond that.

She stared blearily at the small, analog clock next to the bed. It was much later than she'd planned.

After dressing and trying hopelessly to page through one of the books her cousin had provided, she had almost no time to get to class. She vanished from the stoop outside her front door and reappeared on a blessedly empty street not far from the school. She did everything short of run as she made her way to Room 212, which was almost full by the time she slipped into the desk next to Aurelia.

Corinne scowled at her from a few seats away, but Aurelia smiled and arched an eyebrow at her breathless appearance. "You don't have to rush, you know. Patten is always a little late."

Chloe tried to return the smile. Her heart was pounding and she was sure her face looked flushed; not the best choice for fitting in seamlessly. "Oh. Well, you know . . . didn't want to stand out as the new girl."

Aurelia shrugged, her eyes flitting over Chloe's new splint. "Was that a doctor's appointment you rushed off to yesterday?"

She nodded, about to pounce on the perfect cover story, when their teacher shuffled into the room, followed by the last stragglers. Their arrival effectively ended the conversation: the room hushed as Mrs. Patten took her place at the front of the class.

After finishing a few announcements, Mrs. Patten sat down at her desk, allowing her students free reign until the bell released them to first period.

As the chatter began to rise, Chloe could hear Corinne faux-whispering to her redheaded friend, Heather.

"God, who would *wear* that?" Her gaze fell pointedly on Chloe's blasé sweater/skirt combo. The sweater was an especially chunky one she'd been proud of the night before. But as a bead of sweat rolled down her back and the whispers grew, she began to rethink that decision.

"Right?" Heather shrieked, turning to get the attention of another girl sitting nearby and pointing toward Chloe.

"I guess revenge begins early," Aurelia remarked, glancing toward Corrine and Heather.

"Revenge?" Chloe asked.

"You know, for yesterday," she responded slowly. "That kind of thing is a big deal."

"Oh. Oh right, yesterday." Corrine's threat surfaced in Chloe's mind.

Aurelia grinned. "Better you than me."

But aside from the snide remarks, Chloe didn't notice much of a change in Corrine's behavior. Though it was possible she just wasn't paying attention in the right places. Several times during their first few hours, Aurelia blanched when they passed groups of girls whispering loudly in the hallway.

"Did you hear that?" she'd hiss to Chloe. "That was . . . that was *low*."

None of it particularly concerned Chloe, even when Aurelia repeated some of the less vulgar remarks. Attacks via gossip felt fairly harmless compared to attacks by an angry supernatural. Even practice battles with her cousins, both expert knife wielders, gave her more anxiety than the foul commentary Corrine was spreading.

She started to tell Aurelia something similar, but upon re-alizing how out of place it would sound, finished lamely with, "Yeah, my family used to give me a pretty hard time. I'm the youngest."

Aurelia gave her a sympathetic look. "Sorry," she said, cringing as another group passed them. This time, she didn't call attention to what they'd been saying.

The main problem with day two, as far as Chloe was concerned, was Roger. As it turned out, he shared several classes with her and Aurelia. Yesterday, she'd barely noticed the gawky kid, but today, he was everywhere. When he could, he took a seat next to her or Aurelia, trying to instigate painfully awkward small talk.

By the time gym rolled around, his attempts at flirting—each more uncomfortable than the last—had progressed to a show of would-be macho stretching not far from them, and Chloe was having second thoughts about saving his face from getting smashed in.

"Should've let them do it," she murmured, shaking her head as Roger flexed his zero-percent muscle mass into a calf stretch.

Aurelia snorted with laughter at the same time a student took a basketball to the back of the head, courtesy of Derek. She quickly tried to hide her reaction when the gym teacher shot her a foul look. "Whoops, bad timing . . . anyway, I wouldn't worry about Roger. He'll calm down after the Spring Fling."

Chloe leaned out over her legs in a deep stretch. "Spring Fling?"

"I forgot, you wouldn't know! It's getting really close now . . . it's kind of the biggest dance of the year. The senior part, especially. Normally, all of the dances are held . . . well, here," Aurelia motioned around the gym as she elaborated, "but when you're a senior, they hold a special Spring Fling for you off campus."

"Oh, yeah?" Chloe asked blandly, stretching an arm across her chest while Aurelia balanced on one leg.

"Yeah, it's going to be amazing this year," Aurelia continued, missing Chloe's complete lack of interest. "I was on the dance committee when they were picking locations—it's these great botanical gardens just north of here. Everyone goes all out for the dance. It's why they're acting the way they are. You know, Corinne and Roger and everyone."

Chloe offered her a blank stare as she switched arms.

Aurelia let out an exasperated sigh. "You *know*. Corinne is trying so hard to be nasty to you, and get everyone on board with that, because she's been campaigning since, like, freshman year to be voted senior Spring Fling Queen."

"Blech," Chloe replied, wrinkling up her nose. "Are people actually going to *vote* for her?"

The other girl shrugged. "Eh, probably. Part of the school thinks she's awesome, part is absolutely terrified of her, and part just doesn't care. Basically, she has the crown in the bag. Unless," she added pointedly, "they find someone else they like more."

"Oh," Chloe replied. A blush warmed her cheeks. She didn't want to become a rallying point for oppressed human teenagers. "Okay, so, then Roger. Why is he so geared up about the dance? He doesn't strike me as the type to be excited for something like that."

Aurelia chuckled. This time, no one was meeting any sort of misfortune and it went by unnoticed. "Oh, Roger. Well . . ." she glanced over at him, watching as he unsuccessfully tried to make a basket with one of the more beaten-in balls, ". . . he's probably vying for a date."

"What?" Chloe exclaimed, dropping the act of stretching altogether.

"You are his savior, after all," the girl said with a shrug and a wry smile.

"Ugh," was her only response.

ॐ

Chloe's lack of work was her second problem with the day. Not school work, of course, but the work her family expected of her. The fact that she'd retained nothing from her early morning page-through of Rus's books left her with little to pursue when it came to Aurelia.

She did, however, do as Alex instructed, and during passing-time between classes, she made an effort to pause and stretch out her senses, searching for any presence that was more than human. Once or twice, she thought she felt a few, but their auras were faint and distant, easily chalked up to the proximity of the school to Molton's supernatural-filled urban landscape.

So instead, she contented herself with what she supposed was typical human conversation. There was no prying or questioning outside of what was socially acceptable, and Chloe realized that she actually got along quite well with Aurelia. The girl was witty and laid back; had the circumstances been different, she imagined they could have actually been friends, whatever that meant.

Most of their lunch—at the same kitschy soup place as the day before—was spent discussing the pros and cons of various subjects for their chemistry assignment: create a project that demonstrates chemistry in everyday life and explain the properties behind it.

Aurelia's initial suggestion was that they try to tackle Micro Gastronomy, a particularly pretentious-sounding form of cooking. However, after Chloe admitted to being useless at both chemistry and cooking, she scaled back to making a cake and talking about how each ingredient made the final product possible.

After lunch, they headed back to school early—at Aurelia's prodding—so they could swing by the library. As they walked, the conversation drifted back toward the Spring Fling dance.

"You know, that Roger kid is pretty eager to go. I'm sure if you threatened someone, too, he'd be all over you," Chloe teased. Aurelia gave an exaggerated mock-cringe.

"Blech, no thank you," she added with a headshake and a giggle. "Though, I wouldn't mind having a date to the dance. Maybe Roger wouldn't be so bad; he looked pretty limber when he was stretching."

Chloe snorted. "If you say so. But seriously, you should be able to get a date. It can't be that hard." Aurelia was attractive by human standards; petite, well-groomed. Her wide, gray eyes made her stand out, certainly, but Chloe couldn't picture that as a bad thing.

Aurelia shrugged. "I don't know. Maybe I'm just shy." Her tone, however, suggested otherwise. Chloe wondered if perhaps it was the same reason that caused the girl's lack of true friends—people avoiding her for reasons she couldn't begin to fathom.

She wanted so badly to tell her it wasn't her fault humans avoided her. But Naimei rules and a lack of the reason *why* Aurelia was far from normal kept her lips shut.

Aurelia was quick to recover, though. She shot Chloe a smirk as they neared the school, turning onto the block by the grand, front entrance. "What about you? Got a fancy homeschool boy to bring?"

Chloe shrugged. She hadn't had much dating experience. It was limited to a few failed relationships with some of the more civil shifters she'd met, and one very poor excuse for flirtation with a human who'd been particularly in tune with the magical side of things. None had lasted long, and none had really mattered. Naimei were traditionally promised to other Naimei, so the process of dating was a pointless exercise in rebellion.

Without making an awkward phone call to a Naimei family abroad, there was no one Chloe could bring. And even with that, there was no one she would *want* to bring.

Before she could answer even somewhat truthfully—a boyfriend in Canada, maybe—they were in front of the school. The weather was fairly good; a great deal of students were milling about outside, chatting in small groups before the bell rang. Most were staring at the newcomer leaning against the dark motorbike parked on the street.

Chloe's gaze had caught him as they rounded the corner. She took in his posture, his dark leather jacket, and felt her eyes widen, a ton of bricks falling hard into her stomach.

It was him. Without a doubt, he was the flash she'd been seeing out of the corner of her eye for weeks. She was one hundred percent sure. And as he raised a hand to rake some of his softly tousled, brown locks out of his eyes, she was also one hundred percent sure he was a vampire.

Aurelia let out a low whistle as she became aware of the stranger. Had the situation been different, Chloe might have felt the same way; he was certainly good-looking, and definitely not a high school student. His skin was tan for a vampire, and his tall form was lean without being gangly.

A group of giggling girls near a row of benches were trying to edge their way closer, completely oblivious to the fact they were inching their way toward a predator. Worse yet, their attempts at subtlety were failing miserably.

Chloe froze. She wasn't sure what to do; she hadn't thought to bring a weapon to school. She was competent when it came to physical combat, and, of course, could always tap into the many offensive or defensive enchantments, but that would require a great deal of effort and was certain to draw more attention than she'd want if she were to stay at Molton Area High School.

As soon as she stopped walking, the vampire smiled. It was a wide, toothy grin that thrummed at her nerves, funneling anxiety into adrenaline. He bobbed his head in a nod and waved at her.

"You *know* him?" Aurelia hissed in her ear.

"Uh . . . kind of," Chloe replied quietly, wondering how he planned to play out this charade.

She thought she heard Aurelia mutter something about needing to try homeschooling, but she couldn't be positive. Moving forward made her head spin. She prayed the vampire was only after her and was not, as Alex had feared, another force interested in Aurelia's mysterious powers.

As Chloe approached, Aurelia at her heels, the vampire's toothy smile settled into a confident smirk.

"Hello," he said, his voice smooth and easy.

"Hi," she replied tersely.

He tilted his head to the side, looking her over with his dark eyes. "Did you get the gift I left you?"

Her eyes narrowed. "That was you?"

His expression stayed innocent. "I thought you'd like it. You didn't?"

"What, did you send her flowers?" Aurelia cut in.

The vampire's gaze jerked to the momentarily forgotten girl, his expression bemused. "Something like that. Though, apparently, the gift was not to Chloe's liking."

She shivered as her name fell from his lips. She'd read about ancient cultures that believed all power lay in a name; giving it out to strangers was as good as laying down to die. She now perfectly understood the desire not to have a potential enemy use something as personal as a name.

She struggled to respond. "Thank you" sounded too grand for someone who'd only been able to return her knife because he'd been following her.

"Look, I know you're probably mad at me." He crossed his arms over his chest, looking down as he kicked at a stone with one dark-brown boot. "But I'd like to make it up to you." When he looked up, his expression could only be described as "puppy dog".

"Oh yeah?" Chloe said, despite herself. "How are you going to do that?"

A corner of his lip jerked upward. Apparently, she'd given the reaction he wanted. "Meet me at Ducante's. Tonight."

"That's a bar!" Aurelia spluttered, her eyes wide.

The vampire looked like he was suppressing a laugh. "It is. But I'm thinking our girl here will be able to get in."

"I really don't think I would," Chloe said quickly. Meeting a vampire at a bar was certainly not the most dangerous thing she could do. But it was far from the least.

"Oh, come on, now," he said easily, shaking off her rebuff. "I'll even leave your name with the bartender."

"I . . . well . . ." she looked hopelessly at Aurelia. She tried to force all her thoughts toward the girl, imploring her to argue, to demand that Chloe help her with their project tonight. Anything that would give her an excuse not to meet with her potentially deadly, vampire stalker on *his* terms.

Aurelia's powers, however, were not working. That, or she was very good at ignoring them, because she took a step forward and gushed: "She'd love to go!" before adding in an undertone, "Don't worry about the project, Chloe."

The vampire grinned. "Fantastic. Eight o'clock, then, we'll say. Ducante's." He took a step closer, leaning forward so that his lips almost brushed Chloe's hair as he said quietly, "Just ask for Josef."

His breath felt icy on her skin. He gave her a wink before swinging a leg over the motorbike, kicking it to life and pulling the handlebars around to zoom off down the street.

It was only then, as a wave of dizziness passed over her, that Chloe realized she'd been holding her breath.

≈

Aurelia practically exploded once Josef was gone. To her, he was not a threatening presence; he was simply an attractive guy chasing Chloe, and as a friend, she wanted to know everything. She bombarded Chloe with questions, everything from how they'd met to why the nature of their relationship earned him Chloe's chilly response.

The answers she gave were almost exclusively lies. She didn't like answering that way; it was easier to keep stories straight if they had a basis in reality. But where Josef was concerned, her reality consisted of two facts: he was a vampire, and he'd been following her for weeks. Neither was suitable to tell Aurelia.

"So, he's obviously older, right? Like a college guy or something?" She pressed as they assembled Bunsen burners in Chemistry.

"Uh, something like that," Chloe replied. That, at least, was sort of true. Josef definitely felt older than most of the vampires she'd ever hunted. He was certainly older than Sam. It was a wonder she hadn't felt his presence, but maybe that came with age. Staying hidden was probably how he'd lived so long.

"You so would be dating a college guy," Aurelia sighed, picking up a graduated cylinder. A smile crept onto her lips. "Did you see Corinne's face?"

Corinne, apparently, had been standing just to the side of the giggling pack of girls on the bench. She and Heather had been loudly vocalizing their opinions on college parties between elaborate hair tosses; an awkward activity, since Heather had very little hair to toss.

When Josef had refused to look at them, her attempts became more desperate, and when he'd waved to Chloe . . . well, then she'd simply been crestfallen.

The disappointment had turned to anger, and anger had turned to intended violence in the hallways. Chloe was sure the enraged blonde had attempted to body check her into a locker, but she'd dodged easily, having been in no mood to play with bruised teenage egos.

"But you're going to go, right?" Aurelia was continuing. "You have to. A date at a real bar . . ." She sounded envious.

"I doubt it'll be anything to write home about," Chloe replied gruffly, stirring the contents of a beaker.

"Whatever, Ducante's looks awesome."

"You know where it is?" Chloe asked, surprised. Most vampire bars she'd been to were dives. Humans were scarce, and those present were all very aware of the sort of creatures they were around.

"Of course," Aurelia said, listing off an intersection. "It's right by this sushi place my parents took me to when I turned sixteen."

When she said the streets, Chloe could dimly picture the bar. It was in the middle of downtown, surrounded by chic restaurants and designer boutiques. Hard to imagine a vampire dive there.

"So," Aurelia gushed. "What are you going to wear?"

SEVEN

Chloe spent several hours of the afternoon pacing her living room, trying to decide what to do. Almost immediately, she ruled out going to her family. It was an unspoken rule among the Naimei that if you couldn't fix a situation on your own, you told someone right away. Being followed was certainly a situation, and being followed for this long without saying anything . . .

No, she couldn't tell her family about Josef; aside from being angry, they would take away her ability to deal with him, chalking it up as one more thing she couldn't handle.

Who to tell, then? Aurelia would have been a good option, but what she already knew was all she could know.

Sam might also be a good confidant. He surely wouldn't be concerned for her well-being, but he could, perhaps, illuminate the situation a bit more. Maybe he would even recognize Josef's name, if they ran in the same circles.

But just as she was settling on him as her best option, she realized she had no idea how to get a hold of him. A frustrated groan followed that revelation and she flopped onto the couch, glaring at the ceiling. At 7 p.m., she retreated to the closet.

She wasn't concerned about her outfit passing as twenty-one year old appropriate. That wouldn't be hard. She was more concerned about it being both inconspicuous for a night in a bar and easy to fight in. As with any date, she had no idea what Josef's true intentions were.

With that stipulation in mind, she passed over the rows of stacked stilettos and delicate kitten heels. She paused at a pair of embellished ballet flats, but in the end, selected a pair of over-the-knee boots in a soft, black leather. She pulled them over dark-washed, skinny jeans, and paired the lot with a long, satin blouse and her trusty, dark leather jacket. It might have been too soon in their relationship for matching outfits, but leather jackets were just so functional. She couldn't help that.

She stashed her favorite knife up her sleeve, but ensured that another two were also on her person; one at her waist, hidden beneath the shirt, and another tucked into the top of her boot. She wouldn't be caught unprepared for whatever the night had in store.

After smearing her eyes with a thick line of kohl, she left the house. The analog clock over the door read an acute 7:30 p.m.; she was running right on time.

It was fifteen minutes to the nearest edge of downtown Molton. She kept her eyes open for Sam, the only familiar face she was interested in spotting, but he didn't appear before she reached the lamp-lit street.

Using her vanishing act was pointless on a night like tonight; appearing breathless in front of the bar would be an obvious sign of weakness, and she had no idea what she was walking into. She raised one hand and hailed a cab, listing off the inter-section Aurelia had mentioned.

The bright yellow taxi slowed to a stop in the area she'd expected. She passed a pile of crumpled bills to the driver as she clambered out of the car and surveyed the area. Ducante's was situated on the bottom floor of a squat, brick building, sandwiched between two others housing restaurants. Large windows showcased well-dressed diners enjoying the restaurants' fare, while Ducante's, on the other hand, had narrow, frosted windows that gave her no read on what she'd find inside. The wooden door, though gleaming with polish, looked utterly foreboding.

Chloe took a deep breath as she gripped the handle and tugged it open.

Whatever she'd been expecting was far from what Ducante's had to offer. The interior looked more like a speakeasy during the 20's than a modern bar for supernaturals, if one could even consider it that. It was dimly lit by a shimmering chandelier in a cozy, relaxing way. Dark, wooden tables were scattered over glowing hardwood floors. And booths, populated mostly by humans, lined the walls. She picked out a few shifters, one vampire, but for the most part, the mortals seemed unaware that Ducante's was anything other than an upscale, *human* establishment.

A long, curved bar swept around the left side of the room, a massive, gilded mirror glittering behind it. Row upon row of top-shelf liquors stood in front of the mirror, reflecting into infinity. The bartender was leaning back against the shelves, lazily polishing a wine glass. And somewhere in the background, the faint sound of jazz drifted through a sound system.

Josef was nowhere in sight.

Chloe approached the bar, pulling back a stool. The polished wood was rimmed with a thick, bronze edge that seemed to glow from years of care. She frowned at it as she took a seat.

Despite its shine, the bronze was speckled with dark streaks she recognized all too well; an extra additive in the alloy all Naimei were allergic to. She felt confident that resting her jacketed arms on the edge wouldn't be a problem, but she kept her bare hands safely on the wood of the bar.

The fact the metal was present made her fear exposure more than usual. Whatever the human element may have said about the bar, the person running it certainly catered to a supernatural clientele. *And* knew how to deal with them.

The bartender squinted at her as she sat down. He had a young-looking face, but his light brown locks were streaked with premature gray. Given the environment and mood of the place, it gave him a distinguished look, especially paired with the white button-up and slacks she assumed was a uniform.

He set the glass he'd been polishing down and made his way casually to her end of the bar.

"What're you drinking?" he asked as he scanned her with his dark, brown eyes. She wondered vaguely which he was trying to measure: her age or what she was.

"Uh," she stalled. She wasn't much of a drinker. "Gin and tonic, I guess."

The bartender smiled. "Sure." He turned to grab a bottle, a cup, some ice. "We don't get a lot of your type in here."

"What's that, pretty girls?" Chloe asked with a wry smile.

"No," he said, turning around as he poured the gin and twisted open a small bottle of tonic. He scanned the room for a moment, ensuring every other customer was occupied before he looked back at her and lowered his voice. "I mean, we don't get a lot of Naimei."

Chloe was glad she didn't have her drink yet; she probably would have choked. She'd expected him to call her a witch, like Sam, maybe, but to name her exactly what she was . . . that was unbelievable.

"What . . . ? How did you . . . ?" She swung her head from side to side, looking desperately at the other customers. None, not even the lone vampire and smattering of shifters, seemed to have noticed the strange word that had fallen from the bartender's lips.

Everyone was continuing their conversations as if nothing happened.

Abandoning her half-made drink for a moment, he leaned across the bar, beckoning her forward. Chloe leaned in hesitantly as the bartender raised one finger to his lips in a hushing gesture. His eyes, formerly dark brown, slid to a bright red color.

Chloe jumped backward so quickly she slapped her right hand on the metal edge of the bar. A crimson blotch instantly appeared on her palm and she cursed, snatching the half-made gin and ice and pressing it to the injury.

She'd never met a demon before.

Full-blooded demons were about as rare as the Naimei. According to the stories, they had a nasty habit of killing each other, as well as just about anything else they could find.

Violent streak aside, though, demons were more like Naimei than either side would like to believe. They had a magic all their own and were equally as difficult to detect. The only traits Chloe'd been taught to look for were the characteristic red eyes and incredibly sharp teeth, but both seemed to be fairly easy to hide, if the demon in front of her was any indication.

"You're . . . you're a . . ."

He smiled an even, human-like smile as his eyes slid back to brown. "*I* am Gregory Ducante, and this is my bar. One of several, in fact, but this location is one of my particular favorites." He winked as if nothing about this was out of the ordinary and plucked the drink from her hands, pouring the second half of tonic in it before setting it back on the bartop.

Chloe's eyes widened. "But . . . but you're a . . . !"

Ducante rolled his eyes and pushed her drink toward her. "Come on, now. Just because I am what I am doesn't mean I can't be a successful business owner. I've found capitalism is the easiest way to ensure absolute chaos."

She downed half her drink before setting it back on the counter, suspicious disbelief still plastered on her face.

"Oh, come on, Naimei," Ducante said lightly, picking up a bar rag and wiping absently at an imaginary spot on his flawless countertop. "Surely you don't believe all the stories. We're not *all* bad, you know."

"Chloe," she said finally, taking another sip of her drink. There were humans in the bar; perhaps what he was saying had some merit. "My name is Chloe."

"Well, Chloe. It certainly is nice to meet you," he said, sinking into a deep mock-bow. "Are you enjoying my humble establishment?"

She bit her lip. "Well . . . yes, I suppose. It's nice," she admitted, before adding, "But . . . I . . . well, I wasn't expecting any of this."

He grinned at her. "And what were you expecting? Typical bar or supernatural hell-hole?"

"Uh, the second one," she said into her drink.

Ducante chuckled. "They really are awful, aren't they? The idiots that run them have absolutely no idea what they're doing."

"Are you . . . are you saying . . . they're all run by . . . ?"

"Oh, heaven's no!" he said, tossing the bar rag aside and grabbing a glass to make himself a drink. "But if they were, they might be better run. No, all of those bars, they limit their clientele. What's the fun in that? How do they learn anything?"

Chloe leaned over to snag a lime from his side of the bar. "So . . . you open your bar up to everyone. And then what?"

He grinned, pouring liquid from an unlabeled bottle into his glass. It was a dark burgundy. "And then I sit back and collect my money. Or sometimes, things more valuable than money," he added with a wink.

She frowned, squeezing the lime into the final sips of her drink. "How did you know what I was?"

Ducante shrugged as he took a long swig from his glass. Chloe cringed as she tried not to imagine what the mystery liquid could be. "I saw you give the counter the eye, and then you confirmed my suspicions."

Her gaze traveled down to the glowing bronze. "Did . . . did you put this here on purpose? To . . . identify people?"

His grin widened. "Well, of course, my dear Chloe. I like to know who is in my bar, after all."

"Do you have things like that set up for everyone?" she asked.

"Of course," he said again, and tilted his glass back ever so slightly. The bottom was rimmed with silver, curving about a half inch up the sides. "Vampires, for example, need to be very careful when drinking in this bar."

"Oh," was all she could think to say.

"There are other . . . measures, in place, as well." Ducante shrugged. "Nothing that any successful businessman wouldn't have thought of."

Chloe downed the last of her drink.

"So," he began again, "what brings a Naimei into my bar this evening?"

She frowned. His comment brought her back to the present and the familiar brick of ice settling in her stomach. "Oh. I'm supposed to be meeting . . . Josef, here."

Ducante nearly choked on his mouthful of burgundy liquid. "You're here to meet *Josef*?"

Chloe fidgeted uncomfortably. "Yes?"

Ducante laughed. "Well, you're certainly not his usual taste in girl, but . . . well, I suppose Josef can change after all these years." He shook his head, still chuckling to himself.

"Excuse me?"

"So sorry to inform you, my dear. But take solace that he left a message for you." Ducante cleared his throat before continuing, "He wanted you to meet him 'where the hunt ended.'"

She sat back, crossing her arms. "That doesn't make any sense. He told me to meet him here."

"And he told *me* to tell you that." Ducante smirked, taking another sip of his drink. "I'm going to say you're probably in the wrong place, darling."

"It still doesn't make sense," Chloe repeated, shaking her head as she racked her brain for possible locations. The being followed feeling *had* started around the time of her last hunt. *Was he there?*

Her arm gave a phantom pang. It seemed to know where she needed to go, even if she didn't want to believe it.

"How much do I owe you for the drink?" she asked, slipping off the barstool.

"Today, it's on the house," he said, blowing a kiss in her direction. "Please give Josef my well-wishes."

Chloe rolled her eyes, but nonetheless offered a small wave as she left the bar.

In no time at all, she'd brought herself to the edge of the forest that bordered her house; she wasn't bothering to conserve her energy, because now, she was mad. The adrenaline was enough fuel to get her where she needed to go with momentum to spare.

Not only had Josef followed her for weeks, but now, when he'd come out into the open, he was still toying with her. She moved as quickly as she could while still keeping relatively quiet.

The destination he'd alluded to could only be the scene of her last fight—her final, failed hunt.

Yet, when she entered the clearing, it was completely and utterly empty. She stepped silently into its center: there was no sound now except her near-silent breath.

And then, in all too familiar fashion, a twig snapped.

Chloe whirled around, the knife that had been hidden up her sleeve already in her grip, and placed one hand firmly on the chest of the vampire before her. Josef looked just as he had outside the high school: calm, poised, an air of self-satisfaction. Even with her knife already hovering over his heart.

"Who are you and why have you been following me?" she hissed, eyes narrowed.

"Whoa, whoa!" he said in mock surprise, raising his hands above his head innocently. "Easy there, Princess. I've seen you fight before. I'm not quite sure I'm ready for us to get that close, yet." A small smile curved his lips upward.

She gritted her teeth, twisting the knife point down harder until he cringed: the silver had worked its way through his shirt to meet skin. "Who. Are. You."

He frowned and pushed the knife away, gently, but firmly. "We already went over this. My name is Josef; but you can refer to me as a concerned citizen."

Chloe took several steps back. "I should kill you where you stand for what you've been doing to me. What you're *still* doing to me. Why did you send me to that bar if you weren't even going to be there?"

To her surprise, he chuckled. "Ducante's?" Chloe glared as he continued, "Well, did you meet Gregory? What did you think of him?"

She stayed silent, partially out of spite, and partially because she wasn't sure she had an answer to give. She was still confused about what to make of Ducante, and Josef's behavior wasn't helping her to process.

"He could be a useful friend for you," Josef said, rubbing at the spot on his chest where her knife had touched.

"And how would *you* know that?" she spat, tightening her grip on her blade.

He smiled. "Well, aside from the fact I've been watching you for some time. . . I know what you're trying to do."

Chloe narrowed her eyes. "And what might that be?"

Josef gave a would-be innocent shrug. "I'm assuming the names Pan and Damonos mean something to you?"

"What do you know about that?" she hissed. And what could he possibly know about her very minimal involvement?

"Oh, the usual," he said with a grin. "I know they were the first of the demons. Deadly, dangerous, wild. I know they spawned half of all the modern supernaturals: weres, shifters, vampires. Not unlike how *your* ancestors gave the world the first witches, psychics, and elementalists."

Hearing him list off the information casually, information that had been almost entirely lost to the other races, that no one but her kind should know, made her hair stand on end.

"I also know," he added, "that right now, at this moment, someone is trying very hard to bring them back into the world."

Chloe took that moment to pounce. She didn't know what his game was, but from what he was saying, there was little to no chance he worked for the forces of good and balance. Killing or capturing someone involved could only better her standing with the family.

She hadn't even landed a blow before she found herself on the ground, Josef kneeling over her, one forearm pressed to the base of her throat. He was much faster than she'd anticipated.

"Easy, Naimei," he said coolly. "There's no need for that."

She struggled against him before resigning herself to be still. She met his eyes—his dark, vampire eyes—when she spoke. "Who's trying to bring them back, exactly?"

He made a small tsk-ing noise, raising his other hand to give her a tut-tut-ing gesture. "Now, that I can't tell you. I *can* tell you, however, that his motivations are selfish and far from realistic," Josef climbed to his feet, holding out a hand to help Chloe up, "and they will fail. Pan and Damonos are from an ancient, lawless world. They'll destroy us all if the thought catches their fancy."

Chloe ignored his hand and clambered to her feet of her own accord. Aside from her pride, she was uninjured. "Why are you telling me this?"

Again, Josef shrugged. "Like I said, I'm a concerned citizen. And you need to know—that girl you're chasing, she's only a part of the bigger picture. And a fairly unimportant one at that."

He knew about Aurelia. Chloe felt her blood run cold as she opened her mouth, searching for something to say that might refute his statement, but nothing came. *A fairly unimportant one at that,* she turned it over in her head. Somewhere in the recesses of her brain was a vindicated feeling. She'd been right all along.

"Don't misunderstand—it would still be devastating if she fell into the wrong hands. There are no other eyes on her, though—not yet." His tone dropped to one much more serious than he'd used so far. "But there will be. And when that time comes, it may be too late."

"I . . . so . . . what am I supposed to do?" Her voice was quiet now. She couldn't believe she was asking that question of a vampire. But if, by some chance, he was telling the truth . . .

Josef fixed her with a serious look and she was amazed at the transformation in his expression. His dark eyes appeared deeper somehow. "Exactly what you've been doing, but more. There are pieces of the puzzle that have yet to be uncovered by either side, and you will need to get there first if you're to be successful."

"I . . ." she shook her head, trying to clear it. His request was as vague of those from her family. "Is this why you've been following me?"

"Indirectly," he offered, giving his hand a wave to indicate the unimportance of her question. The gesture screamed *Alex*. Chloe felt her fingers twitch tighter on her knife.

"And where will you be, while I'm sorting through this mess?" she demanded.

His eyes widened in faux-shock. "Well, I'll be right where I've always been: not very far off at all." He gave her a wink.

Her eyes narrowed. "Who are you working for? Who put you up to this?"

He tsk-ed her again, shaking his head back and forth. "No, Chloe, no. This doesn't work like that."

"But—" Before she could get the words out, Josef had closed the gap between them.

"Truth be told . . . well, I might have wanted to find you anyway. Even if I wasn't getting paid." He raised one hand, gently caressing the side of her face. Chloe was too shocked to move.

Abruptly, he turned and vanished into the forest, quicker than a shot, leaving her alone in the clearing. The icy burn from his touch rapidly spread through her body in a way she didn't quite understand.

EIGHT

She wasn't sure how long she stayed in the clearing, staring at the place Josef had vanished. But eventually, something in her seemed to snap to attention and she found the energy to stumble home, the past few hours twisting and turning in her mind.

The impending return of Pan and Damonos wasn't news, but the seriousness of the threat was. Alex and Rus certainly hadn't seemed that concerned. But then again, maybe they were too confident it would be an easy fix. Too confident that, for a Naimei, everything was an easy fix.

Aurelia's lack of discovery was a plus, but the thought of trying to unravel the girl's secrets in some sort of high-stakes, supernatural race filled her stomach with lead.

That was assuming Josef had been telling the truth, though. He knew too much to be making things up, but what was his real motivation for seeking her out? The fact he was being paid to follow her by a mysterious force was not to be overlooked.

And the way he'd left . . .

Well, that was the least of her concerns.

She stumbled up the steps to her front door. Not bothering to try and reach her bedroom, she collapsed on the overstuffed couch and pulled a pillow over her head, immediately diving into sleep.

æ

"Mikhail!" she shrieked, racing into the kitchen, the quilted blanket clutched tightly in her grasp.

Something was wrong with the room. It seemed darker, the shadows in the corners more menacing, as if they could reach out and grab her.

Lightning split the darkness. There was a peal of thunder fast on its heels, but not the normal sort. This thunder was deeper, angrier, more intense.

Her foot caught on the edge of the blanket. She sprawled on the kitchen floor, looking up at her brother; he stood, his back to her, hands gripping the countertop as he gazed out the window.

He turned.

His eyes were bright red, his teeth too sharp . . .

æ

She woke screaming. Disoriented, she thrashed against the mess of pillows before remembering she'd fallen asleep on the couch. *Her* couch. In the small, sunlit living room of her cozy house in Molton.

She sat still for a moment, squeezing the edge of a pillow for comfort, waiting for her heart rate to return to normal. She sighed and ran a hand through her hair, glancing up at the clock.

It was almost ten in the morning.

At first, she didn't register what that meant, but as her recent obligations came rushing back, she let out a mumbled curse. She was late for school. Grudgingly, she got up to seek a change of clothes and a shower.

Despite what she'd learned the night before, she couldn't bring herself to feel any sense of urgency. She took her time getting ready and started walking toward school. It would have been a long and tiring trek for a human, but to Chloe, it could barely be considered exercise. She chose the most meandering route possible, passing areas of town she rarely traveled in, hoping to run into someone she could talk to.

Her head felt too full, her body sluggish from all that had happened. As she walked, though, she realized there was no one—in Molton or otherwise—that would fit *that* role.

Her family seemed out of the question at this point. She had no idea how to explain that she'd decided to meet, on her own, with a vampire who'd been following her for weeks. Oh, but the upside? She was still alive and he seemed to have a lot of information about the situation they were dealing with. Maybe he was even the one behind it.

If she went to them now, they'd be more furious than grateful. They undoubtedly knew more than they alluded to, so Josef's news probably wouldn't even be news to them. And if it was, they'd expect her to be able to produce her vampire source. She doubted he would be tracked down easily, and even if she could find him, it would be poor repayment for the information he'd given her. No. Her family could work through things on their own.

And maybe she could do the same.

By the time she reached the front entrance of Molton Area High School, she hadn't encountered a single soul aside from the occasional human out on a coffee break.

With a heavy sigh, she made her way through the front doors and into the office.

The gray-haired secretary didn't seem pleased. Apparently, showing up any later than first bell was something one simply *did not do* in high school—or, at least, that's what the woman told her as she tried to scrape together a reason for her tardiness.

It took a lot of persuasion and a small burst of magic, but, in the end, the woman obediently—if not somewhat confusedly—scribbled out a pass. As Chloe accepted it and headed out the door to the hallway, she reflected that perhaps, in her residual anxiety, she'd used a bit too much of her powers: a glance over her shoulder revealed that the woman was scribbling out an entire stack of passes, her eyes slightly crossed.

The unfortunate timing of her morning meant she'd arrived during her Phys Ed period. She entered the gym halfway through the class, not bothering to change into her gym uniform. The majority of the students were playing a skills-based basketball game; Chloe scanned them for the one she was looking for and found Aurelia sitting on the bleachers, tapping her foot anxiously and tugging at her hair. She'd apparently already lost whatever the game was.

"Where were you?" she demanded as Chloe joined her. "I was really worried. I thought maybe something happened on your date. You know, the one at the *bar*."

Chloe had almost forgotten she'd gone to Ducante's, much less under the pretense of a date. She offered a shrug. "No, I don't know. It was fine, I guess. Just a late night."

Aurelia let out an excited squeal. "Oooo, tell me everything!"

"Well . . ." Chloe bit her lip. What could she tell? "I mean . . . it wasn't a big deal, really."

The other girl rolled her eyes. "You just said it was a late night. Come on, spill! Does he kiss as good as he looks?"

"What?" Chloe spluttered. She hadn't been expecting that. But, of course, if Aurelia was believing it was a date . . . "No. I mean, it wasn't like that. That didn't happen."

Aurelia looked disappointed. "Oh. Well, what was the point, then?"

"He . . ." she began, searching for something to use as an explanation, "He just wanted to talk. And for me to meet one of his friends."

"Well, that's a positive sign, right? Meeting friends? Are you going to take him to the Spring Fling?"

"I . . . I don't think he'd be into that," she replied, shifting uncomfortably. "And it's a little too soon for . . . that."

Aurelia had a barrage of follow-up questions prepared and the rest of the day was more or less devoted to answering them. Chloe tried to field them as best she could, struggling to remember the lies she'd told the day before and building on them whenever possible. A few times, she gave an answer that directly contradicted what she'd already said and was forced to back pedal as quickly as she could to correct the situation.

Luckily, Aurelia was eager to live vicariously through someone else—especially someone with an undisputed "hottie". She informed Chloe over lunch that the mystery man on the motorcycle was the hottest gossip in school; some of the bolder girls, Corinne included, were claiming they were the ones he'd come to see, but almost everyone seemed to know it was really Chloe at the center of it.

"Don't you see what this means?" Aurelia squealed as they headed back to class. "If you could have a guy like that on your arm—I mean, you know, if you could convince him to go—you could give Corinne a run for her money for Spring Fling Queen."

Chloe shook her head slowly. The last thing she wanted was to attend a high school dance, much less use it as a platform to compete with a mean-spirited teenager. "I don't know. That seems pretty unlikely. Who is she taking, anyway?"

Aurelia shrugged. "Some jock friend of her brothers, probably. That's who she always ends up taking. Never the most attractive and never the least, but always *very* intimidating to vote against, if you catch my drift."

"Oh. She brings a muscle?"

"Exactly," Aurelia said with a nod. "So, you can see why we have to make you win, right? Think of how great it will be . . . !"

Chloe shook her head again, a small smirk in place. "Who are you taking to the dance?"

The other girl clammed up. As they headed into Chemistry, she quickly changed the subject to a discussion of what they'd need to look for at the library that night.

"And you said Josef had some ideas, right?"

"Oh . . . uh. Yeah. Maybe," Chloe said. She'd gotten caught up in an unexpected question and had admitted Josef wanted to help her with something; it was more information than she'd expected to give, and when the inevitable follow-up question came, she'd blurted out the first human thing she could think of: their chemistry project.

She slid into a seat near the back of the room, not even bothering to take out the notebook she carried around for appearances. The teacher had notes upon notes scrawled across the board, a sure sign he was gearing up for a long lecture.

Across the room, Roger was blatantly ignoring the teacher in favor of staring at her. His gaze was confused and pained at the same time, like someone just kicked his puppy. It made her feel infinitely awkward, but no more so than the previous attempts at small talk and showmanship had.

Well, she mused as Roger let out a particularly heavy sigh. *I guess some good came from Josef coming to school, after all.*

❧

"So, I know we said library right away," Aurelia said as they walked out of the building, "but would you mind swinging by my house on the way? It's really not far off. I just don't want to carry all of *this* around with me." She tapped the heavy bag at her side.

Chloe shrugged. "Sure, doesn't matter to me."

"I don't understand how you're not bringing home a ton of books, too," Aurelia said bitterly, glancing over at Chloe's unencumbered form.

She shrugged again. "I just don't feel like doing homework this weekend." At Aurelia's scandalized expression, she added, "But I'll get it done! Don't worry."

The truth was, she had no intention of getting it done. None of it was difficult, but she had more important things to do with her precious weekend time. A minor enchantment would take care of the teachers, and it wasn't as if her future depended on passing—or even staying in—human high school.

"Whatever," Aurelia commented. She adjusted the bag on her shoulder and led the way through the meandering streets. They pushed past the office buildings and apartments until they reached a row of older homes set very close together.

Aurelia moved purposefully to the one on the corner, leading Chloe up the walk through the small yard.

"Well, this is it," she said, pausing on the front stoop. She bit her lip, looking unsure about what to do next. "I . . . uh. Well. I'm not going to be very long, but . . . you know what, yeah, you can come in if you want. We can grab some food or something."

Chloe tried to give what she hoped was a reassuring smile. "Sure. Sounds good."

Aurelia fumbled with her keys for a moment before pushing open the door.

The inside of her home was what Chloe imagined Alex wanted his apartment to be—so clean, it gleamed. The monochromatic palette combined with the lines and angles of the stylish furniture to give it a cold, unlived-in look. Hardly the typical warm, suburban home.

"I'll be right back," Aurelia called as she headed up a flight of stairs.

Chloe shuffled through the entrance hall into a dining area and a large, sweeping kitchen that was absolutely filled with shining, stainless steel appliances. Adjacent to the kitchen was an open living room with a fireplace, the red brick looking horribly out of place against the austere surroundings. The only thing that looked lively was the series of pictures on the mantel, all in frames that didn't quite match the modern feel of the house. She assumed they were remnants from Aurelia's childhood, from the time before her parents turned into, as she called them, "workaholics".

The photographs were predominantly of a small gray-eyed girl walking through rooms not unlike those Chloe was standing in, though they were filled with much softer, homier-looking furniture. A shot in the middle showed what Chloe assumed to be Aurelia's whole family: Aurelia in the middle, smiling with a mouthful of braces, and a man and woman on either side who looked quite a lot like her.

None of the pictures revealed anything unordinary or gave her any hint of what she should be looking for. She sighed in disappointment.

As the thump, thump, thump, of Aurelia's feet sounded on the stairs, Chloe returned to the kitchen.

"All right. Do you want something to eat?" Aurelia asked,

making her way to the silver fridge. She pulled open the door to reveal a scantily stocked interior. "We have the makings for . . . sandwiches, sandwiches, and more sandwiches," she said with a half-hearted smile.

"Uh . . . I'll take a sandwich," Chloe said tentatively, perching on a chrome bar stool.

"Sorry that's all we have," Aurelia said as she began sorting through ingredients. "I mean . . . my parents travel a lot, I told you that. They just forget that when they're gone, I'm still capable of cooking."

"Yeah, well, mine are the same way," Chloe said, accepting the plate Aurelia passed her. Her parents had cooked before they were gone, of course, but she'd been too young to pick any of it up. The meals she did know how to make—which she could count on one hand—had been bestowed on her by either Mikhail or Rus. "My brother wasn't a bad cook, though. You know, when he was around."

Aurelia nodded as she chewed thoughtfully on her sandwich.

❧

As it turned out, Aurelia's house was almost exactly halfway between the school and the library; it didn't take long to walk to the pleasant, cream-brick building—one of the oldest in town.

"Let's see . . ." Aurelia mused as they entered the lobby. "I'm not exactly sure where the books we're looking for would be. How about this? All the baking stuff is down here; I'll look through that and, at the very least, find us a recipe. Do you want to find the chemistry section and look for books on how baking works?"

"Sure," Chloe replied.

Aurelia took off, heading purposefully down the aisles, leaving Chloe to ponder the section she needed; the library was quite large, and since human books rarely held sway in her dealings, she'd spent little to no time in it. After a quick glance toward the over-bright kids section, she elected to go upstairs, locating the staircase tucked in a back corner.

The second floor was almost more intimidating than the one below it. Downstairs had hosted a nice, open seating area in front of the check-out desks and turning-racks of popular novels. Up here, it was nothing but stack upon stack of shelved books and a tiny area in the middle with a few tables and chairs.

It was more crowded than she would have expected on a Friday night. At least a dozen college-aged humans were meandering the shelves, plucking a book here, a book there. *One of the local schools must be nearing a testing period,* she thought.

The crowds, combined with the narrow halls of books, made her nervous. As she edged between different stacks, praying she was headed for the chemistry section, she found herself reaching out with bits of power to feel her environment.

The results came back monotonously dull: human, human, human, and . . . not so human. In the far corner of the library, if she really stretched, she could feel a presence that was distinctly vampire. And distinctly familiar.

She moved as quickly as she could toward that non-human corner, trying to make sure she wasn't drawing attention to herself in the process. The students at the shelves seemed much too engrossed in their studies to notice a girl sneaking through the vicinity, though.

She paused, one last shelf separating her from the familiar energy. A person stepped out from behind the books.

Thin, pale, dark hair: Sam.

He wiped his mouth with the back of his hand, caught sight of her, and froze.

"You again," he said tartly.

Before she could respond, a dazed human staggered out from the shadows behind Sam. Her light hair was mussed.

Two small punctures in her neck were already beginning to heal.

Sam stared at Chloe as if challenging her.

The rumpled young woman mumbled something indistinguishable before putting on a lopsided smile and stumbling back toward the stairs.

"She'll be fine," Sam muttered once the girl was out of earshot.

Chloe sighed, willing her resolve to stay in place. "At least you don't kill them."

He shrugged.

Since she'd stopped hunting, the feeding habits of vampires had been the last thing on her mind. Now, thrust under a spotlight in front of her, the diet once again seemed savage and cruel. An unsettled feeling crept into her stomach as she thought about the company she'd been keeping, and what they did when they weren't in her presence.

"Were you looking for me, or something?" Sam asked, tilting his head to the side. It was the closest he'd gotten to looking like the earnest boy he'd been when they first met, when he'd seemed almost human.

She clung to the image, willing her stomach to settle. "Indirectly," she answered, her mind drifting involuntarily to Josef.

Sam reached forward, grabbing her wrist, and pulled her between two tall shelves. "Why?" he said seriously. "What's up?"

Chloe shivered. Vampires were always so cold. "I . . . well. I've been looking into that stuff you were worried about."

Suddenly, she was second-guessing his status as a potential confidant. She didn't know him, not really. What was she honestly comfortable telling him? The bare bones, maybe—could she even give that away without revealing herself?

Sam's expression was one of eager anticipation, so she continued, "I went to Ducante's last night."

He raised his eyebrows. "*You* went to Ducante's?" His tone was skeptical.

"Yes," she said defensively, "Why? Do you hang out there a lot?"

Sam shrugged. "Well, here and there. It really fills up on Saturday nights. That's how I heard about all the people getting nervous. And about you."

She frowned. So Ducante undoubtedly knew more about her than he'd let on the night before. "Yeah, well. I can see what you mean. It was . . . well, everyone was like you said. Nervous."

At her half-hearted story, his expression shifted to one of disappointment and suspicion. "That's . . . all? You didn't learn anything new?"

"Did you?" she challenged, putting her hands on her hips.

He shook his head. "No. I mean, everyone still seems upset, like you said. Everything still feels off, and I heard the shifters in town are getting pretty restless. But no one can say why."

"Well—" Chloe was about to offer another tidbit of information, when a new, hushed voice rang out from between the shelves.

"Chloe? Chloe . . . Chloe! Hey, there you are," Aurelia said, shuffling over with an armful of books. "Oh, hello," she added, her eyes widening at the sight of Sam.

"Hi," Sam said with a slight smile, slipping back into his near-human, innocent act.

Chloe cringed. She hadn't wanted Aurelia to meet any other supernaturals—and now, here she was, face to face with her second vampire. At least she was still blessedly ignorant, but at this rate, how long would that last?

"Are you one of Chloe's friends?" Aurelia asked, shifting the pile of books. The title of the topmost one proudly proclaimed: *Baking For Dummies.*

"Uh," Sam said, his eyes flickering to Chloe. She gave him a minute shrug and he continued, "Yeah. Yeah, I just moved to town not too long ago. Met Chloe right when I got here."

"Were you homeschooled, too?" Aurelia said. Chloe siphoned some of the load from the other girl's arms, leaving her with a much smaller stack of literature. Aurelia flashed her a grateful smile.

Sam gave Chloe a curious, sidelong glance before fixing Aurelia with a would-be-genuine smile. "Nah, Chloe and I just always run into each other. How do you two . . . ?" He gave a convoluted wave to indicate the girls.

"School," Aurelia answered lightly, "We both go to Molton. I'm Aurelia, by the way."

"Sam," he replied, reaching out to shake her hand.

Chloe purposefully leaned against a shelf, spilling several books onto the floor. The last thing she needed was to have Aurelia's powers emerge mid-handshake with a vampire. "Oh, whoops. Clumsy me. Aurelia, it looks like you found what we need for our project."

"I . . . yeah," she replied, blinking in confusion at the awkward disruption. "Yeah. I think I have just about everything. The cooking section was definitely well-stocked. What about you, did you find anything worthwhile?"

Chloe shook her head, trying to contort her expression to one of deepest disappointment. "Not really. I mean, the chemistry section was filled with mumbo-jumbo science books; I wouldn't have realized if I *was* looking at something relevant."

Sam squinted at her curiously. At least *that* expression was truly genuine.

Aurelia shrugged. "It's no big deal. I'm pretty sure I got us covered. Hey, but I was thinking, after we check these bad boys out, do you want to go to this ice cream place down the street? I mean, it's Friday night. We should do something sort of fun."

Chloe shrugged. Technically, she did have things to do; research the still-untouched books Rus had given her, for one. But Aurelia had a point: now that she'd stopped hunting, when did she ever do anything fun?

"Sam," Aurelia was saying, a wide smile on her face. "Would you like to come with us?"

Chloe's stomach sank.

"I'd love to," he said with a smile to match Aurelia's.

The ice cream place turned out to be a sweet, little, family-run operation decorated as a 1950's soda shop. Being that it was a Friday, it was filled with families and teenaged couples, some sitting at the candy-colored tables, others spread out along a bar that stretched from the cash register to the other side of the store.

An entire wall was dedicated to bulk candy. Children swarmed around it, begging and pleading with haggard-looking parents.

It was the last place Chloe would've ever expected to see a vampire. But despite her reservations, she found a certain amusement in watching Sam navigate the store—scowling as kids bumped into him, staring bemusedly at the different candy options.

Aurelia and Chloe were, of course, the only ones eating, and at Aurelia's suggestion, they took their single scoops of brightly-colored ice cream to one of the metal tables sitting outside. It was warm for early spring, with just a hint of rain-scent on the air.

Sam, though hardly outspoken, proved to be a semi-competent conversationalist. He kept up with the basic chatter supplied by Aurelia, with occasional questions and prompts from Chloe. Mostly, the topics adhered to ordinary small talk: Aurelia asked about his old school and Sam recited a polite and vague lie.

She talked about the Spring Fling dance, especially after Sam admitted his private school hadn't celebrated it as a high holy day the way public schools did, and eventually moved on to discussing the finer points of why they'd been in the library and what the chemistry project would entail.

"So, Chloe," she said, scraping the last bit of bright purple cream from her cup, "I was thinking that maybe we just research this weekend, and next week we can try to finish everything up?"

"Sure, that works for me," Chloe replied, setting her empty, blue-tinted cup on the table.

"Is that guy going to come help us with the project?" Aurelia said with a smirk.

Chloe frowned. "Who?" She'd almost forgotten the lies she'd woven the last few days.

"You know. *Josef.* The guy who took you to a *bar* last night," Aurelia prodded, her expression scandalized.

She cringed. Sam's eyes had narrowed in her direction; he now knew for sure that she'd been withholding information in the library. She hadn't found Ducante's on her own—she'd been led to it, and she was sure he'd guess it was another vampire she'd been in contact with.

"Wow, Chloe. I didn't know you were going to bars with other guys. That's pretty interesting." He gave a cold smirk. "I bet those guys really *know a lot* about the world, huh?"

"Sam—" she started, ready to apologize, to offer him the information he wanted.

But he was already standing. "Whatever. I should probably be going anyway." He glanced briefly to Aurelia and muttered, "Nice meeting you," before he turned, pushing past a family on their way into the shop and disappeared down the street.

Aurelia frowned and licked her spoon. "That was weird."

Chloe sighed. The girl had no idea.

They lingered at the table for a few more minutes before deciding to call it a night. Chloe insisted on walking Aurelia home, claiming it wasn't far from where she was headed. It took some convincing, but eventually, Aurelia agreed of her own accord, sparing Chloe from having to use enchantments. She really didn't want to; not on Aurelia. But she also didn't want to leave the girl alone quite yet. Sam didn't seem like the vindictive type, but she wasn't taking any chances.

Once they'd said their goodbyes and Aurelia was safely shut inside her perfectly sterile, modern house, Chloe ducked into the shadows of the buildings and pulled herself into the nothingness that would bring her home.

She may very well have alienated one of her only supernatural acquaintances, but for now, that didn't matter. He'd told her exactly where she needed to go—and when—if she wanted to know what he knew.

NINE

Chloe woke early on Saturday, plagued by the same dreams that always haunted her. This time, however, the old memories were altered with new figures: Ducante, in the background, laughed at her ignorance, while Sam stood to the side, arms crossed, steadfastly refusing to speak.

She lay awake in bed, wrapped snugly in her blanket cocoon, reluctant to face the day. When she did finally get up, she puttered from room to room before heading to the kitchen to scrounge up breakfast. The ice box rattled and wheezed as she came near it, the technology pressing uncomfortably against her powers.

Her refrigerator was almost as barren as Aurelia's, but she did manage to find a few eggs hidden on a back shelf, as well as a box of cereal lurking in one of the cabinets. She brought everything to the table and sat, staring grimly at the closed box containing the Ways.

Despite Alex's wishes, she hadn't touched them since his last visit. Using them now would be mildly pointless. She may not know exactly *who* to look for, but she did have an idea where to start. And action had always served her better than study.

As she finished the last of her eggs, she felt a sudden pang of longing for her brother. She rarely missed Mikhail; she was too used to him being gone. But he'd always seemed to operate on her wavelength. For him, an ear to the ground would often yield quicker results than the arduous process of assembling and observing the Ways, even if he claimed otherwise to the family.

He was also the least likely to berate her for keeping so many secrets. She really should have reported Josef to the family, should have brought up the fact there was a demon happily living in Molton under the guise of a bar owner. Rus and Alex wouldn't take either revelation with any semblance of grace. Mikhail, though. If the timing was right, she could tell him.

She sighed, digging out a handful of dry cereal. Retreating to the couch, she pulled one of Rus's hefty books into her lap with a grunt.

The tome was one of the oldest she'd ever opened. Its contents had mostly likely been held in scrolls before a studious Naimei in the Middle Ages had thought to copy and translate the text, magically sealing the pages for future generations. Even so, time had eroded the spells, making the pages feel thin and dry. In some places, the ink had faded or smudged, and Chloe had to squint to read the majority of it.

It was a documentation of Naimei past and supernatural present; histories of the various supernatural lines, including complete family trees that extended almost to present day. The Naimei who'd assembled the book had left several pages in every section blank for future generations to fill in.

Chloe flipped slowly and carefully through the different categories, looking for the section on psychics. She paused on a frail sheet detailing a brief line of Fire Elementals, recognizing the handwriting on the bottom of the page. Mikhail's small, cramped scrawl had made an addition to the text.

"Judd and Everett Agayn," it read. No birthdates, no death dates. Just the names.

She frowned over them for a moment and then shrugged. Whatever the addition meant, it was irrelevant to her search. Aurelia's powers were mysterious and still uncharted, but the extra precaution she showed the Bunsen burner in Chemistry probably meant they didn't have much to do with fire.

She went back to rifling through the pages until she landed on psychics. Her hopes that the section would be illuminating were quickly dashed. There were almost as many types as there were for witches. Psychic abilities were unique in that new ones were always manifesting—some lines even began where others in the book had ended.

Chloe sighed and settled back into the cushions.

The histories of the different lines were interesting, she supposed, but getting through them wasn't easy. The language was dry and stale. Entire sections were written in another language altogether. They weren't hard for Chloe to interpret—over the years she'd become competent, if not fluent, in several languages—but it certainly did slow her down.

There was also the fact that psychic abilities seemed to be a form of magic humans were comfortable with, if not entirely adept at spotting in its true form. They wildly flaunted their abilities, whether real or presumed, and the claimants had been dutifully logged. Until, of course, some of them came out as false. The charts were littered with scribbled-out names of those that, in reality, had just been very intuitive individuals.

It took her so long to sift through the information that, by the time she looked up from the book, it was already early evening. And she was no closer to finding anything about Aurelia or her powers. None of the names matched, and none of the listed traits particularly aligned with what she'd felt that day in school.

Frustrated, she gave up on the book, setting it back in the pile with the others. The sky was showing streaks of red and orange as the evening dwindled, and she had other ventures to fill her night: ones that, hopefully, would be more fruitful than her research.

She rose and headed for the shower. The hot water felt invigorating; exactly what she needed. Though Ducante's had seemed tame during the week, she imagined she'd need to stay alert if she wanted to safely eavesdrop on a Saturday night.

At her closet, she selected a slim-fitting, black dress. It buttoned down the front with a very vintage ruffle that matched the feel of the bar. She shrugged her jacket over the dress and hid her favorite knife up her sleeve, a gesture she hoped would only be precautionary.

She coated her eyes with more dark makeup than she usually wore and set her stick-straight hair in thick, loose curls. She was still recognizable, but she doubted any enemies she still had would be able to place her at first glance. Rolling the sleeve of her jacket up, she carefully removed the Velcro cast. She certainly didn't need to be recognized for an injury, of all things. She shook the sleeve back in place and examined her reflection in the long mirror before heading out the door.

જ

Twenty minutes later, she was outside Ducante's.

The street—not to mention the bar itself—had an entirely different energy. The restaurants on either side were full and lively; people lingered on the sidewalk, caught up in the pleasant conversation a meal and several cocktails brought on. The door of Ducante's was propped open, allowing the swing of Big Band music to spill onto the street. And a black-shirted bouncer was checking I.D.'s as a small queue of people waited to enter.

Chloe slipped into the back of the line. She didn't have an I.D. that would identify her as over twenty-one. In fact, she didn't have an I.D. that would identify her as any age at all; in the human world, she didn't exist. There were, of course, other methods for gaining entry. She took a deep breath, preparing herself as the human couple in front of her went inside.

She stepped up to the bouncer. He squinted at her for a moment and then nodded her through. The spell she'd been gathering was still frozen behind her lips. Chloe frowned, tentatively stretching her power to probe the burly man in front of her.

Witch.

Of course Ducante would hire *witches* as bouncers. They might not have been able to recognize her as Naimei, but they could certainly feel her presence as supernatural. No doubt he was under instruction to let the supernaturals through, as many—vampires especially—wouldn't have valid identification. Sensible though it may have been, it was odd to see a witch working in an establishment like Ducante's. Most of the lines were steadfastly against the darker side of the supernatural world, and even more against mixing that with mortals.

Chloe could recall several lines, though, who were significantly less scrupulous. They would do anything and work for just about anyone, as long as the price was right. The man before her had evidently emerged from one of those.

She gave him a curt nod and slipped into the bar.

Just like the street outside, it felt much different from her last visit. There were certainly more supernaturals; she could feel several vampires mingling with the crowd. One, in her direct line of sight, was sweet-talking a giggling human girl at the bar.

Chloe scowled.

There were also a number of shifters and a few others she couldn't specifically identify. The number of humans in the bar—which was surprising after what Sam had said about the wealth of information found here on the weekend—made things difficult. Their auras muddled the more-than-mortal presences around them.

Most seemed fairly ignorant of what they were surrounding themselves with, while others lingered near vampires in a more knowing way. That was the most frustrating thing about humans: from generations past, they possessed a keen intuition that told them when they were near something dangerous, even if they didn't consciously realize it. Yet so many ignored that feeling, and most could be tricked by a supernatural that played their part well.

When in Rome . . . , she thought.

She sighed and moved to the bar. Gregory Ducante was not behind it, as she'd been expecting; but then, he had mentioned he owned several bars. Maybe he chose not to spend busy Saturday nights at this one. She sipped her drink thoughtfully. It was just as well. She wasn't in the mood to talk—all she wanted to do was listen.

Slowly, she circulated through the room, hovering near large groups. She stayed just close enough to appear like she was involved in the conversation, dissuading other roaming singles from approaching her, but just far enough away that her presence wouldn't be suspicious. It worked fairly well; she was able to eavesdrop on several conversations. But none of them were particularly enlightening. There was a nervous trill to the air, just as Sam had said, but she could easily have chalked it up to the number of people in the bar and the excitement of a Saturday night. The names Pan and Damonos certainly weren't being mentioned; in fact, demons were not a topic of conversation at all.

She'd almost reached the far corner of the bar when a familiar head of shaggy, dark hair caught her eye—Sam. She abandoned the conversation she'd been listening in on—a group of werewolves chatting about the difficulties of hunting near the city, and an especially obnoxious vampire who'd moved through their territory—and crossed to where she'd seen him. She was so sure he'd been talking to the red-headed shifter girl, but when she drew closer, pushing her way through the crowd, the redhead was the only one there. She scanned the room, but Sam, if it had been him, was gone.

Chloe shook her head, swirling the remaining contents of her drink. She was beginning to think the entire night had been a waste when she felt a tap on her shoulder.

She turned around slowly, muscles tensed. She expected to see an angry, wronged vampire, but instead, she faced a pleasant grin.

The man in front of her had tawny hair that fell in waves to his chin. His skin was tanned, and he almost seemed to carry the smell of sunshine and outdoors with him. Chloe might have mistaken him for human at first glance, but his startling gold eyes gave him away. A werewolf—potentially one of the ones she'd been eavesdropping on. Had he noticed? Was that why he was approaching her?

She racked her brain, to trying to place him among the circle she'd been standing near, while innocently sipping her drink. *When in doubt, just play dumb,* Chloe thought.

"I couldn't help but notice you," he said, raising his voice over the noise. "You look too good to be true."

Chloe felt her eyes widen. Not what she'd been expecting. But it could certainly still be a trap. She shrugged, mouthing something about the music being too loud.

"I'm Cain," he said more loudly, holding his hand out to shake.

"What?" she shouted, still pretending not to hear him.

"Cain," he said, pointing to himself.

Chloe shook her head. She could hear him; of course she could hear him. She may not have had the keen hearing of a vampire or a were, but she was still capable of overcoming bar noise. "It's too loud in here. I think I'm going to go—"

"I know your brother," Cain said, his voice quieter now. "I recognized you."

She almost dropped her drink in shock. That *certainly* wasn't what she'd been expecting. "You know . . . ?"

"Mikhail, yeah," he said calmly. He glanced around the bar, and then nodded for her to follow him. Cain weaved his way through the crowd to a large door near the bar marked Staff Only. He casually pushed it open, gesturing for Chloe to slip inside.

She did. He followed behind her, allowing the door to close before flicking a light switch.

They'd entered what appeared to be a storage room. It was no more than a broom closet, really, but lined with boxes, bottles of alcohol, and jars of various garnishes. A large chest freezer was pushed against the back wall.

"You two look a lot alike, you know," Cain said, leaning against one of the shelves. He grabbed a bottle and began absently observing the label. "Uncannily alike. You could be twins."

"Well, we're not. He's—"

"Older. I know." Cain smiled. He had a kind face, the sort that warranted trust all on its own. It made him dangerous. *Attractive.* Chloe forced herself to push the thought away.

"He talks about you quite a bit," he remarked, smoothing a corner of the label with his thumb.

Chloe frowned, leaning against her own shelf. "Oh, yeah? And exactly how do you know my brother?"

He shrugged. "He's helped my pack out a few times. Once with a pack leader who . . . well, let's just say, got too big for his britches." His smile became slightly watery. Werewolves were a prideful group; whatever his pack leader had done, it had reflected badly on the rest of them. "And another time, with a group of shifters who got cheeky."

Somewhere, in the recesses of her mind, Chloe could hear Mikhail—back from one of his long trips—talking about similar situations. "Oh. So . . . you know . . . ?"

"What you are?" Cain replaced the bottle on the shelf and selected another. "In as many words."

She shifted uncomfortably. "So why did you bring me in here? To reminisce?"

After observing the new bottle, Cain unscrewed the cap and took a swig. He pulled a face and quickly placed it back on the shelf. "No, Sweetheart, I pulled you in here because Mikhail mentioned that his younger sister was on a different career path than he was. He said she was hunting," he fixed her with a serious look, "and Ducante's is no place for hunters."

"Well, that's fine. I'm not a hunter anymore," she said coolly.

He rolled his eyes. "Come *on*. Don't give me that. The way you were lurking around out there? It reeked of a predator honing in on its prey."

She felt her heart flutter. Had she been that obvious? "I wasn't hunting. Not for vampires, anyway." She kicked at a piece of plastic wrap on the ground. "I'm looking for information."

Cain raised an eyebrow. It had the slightly cliché effect of making him look like a puppy. "Oh? On what?"

"I . . ." she paused. "I can't really tell you."

He snorted. "Oh, right. You lot and your *secrecy*. You know, your life would probably be easier if you'd just trust people from time to time."

Chloe debated for a moment, and said, "I've heard that . . . that supernaturals have been nervous, lately. About something. I'm just trying to get to the bottom of it."

To her surprise, Cain laughed. "We're *always* nervous."

She fixed him with a quizzical stare, and he elaborated. "There's always something, isn't there? Always someone who wants more power, who thinks they know best. It comes with the territory, so to speak."

"So . . . so no one's been . . . you know, more nervous than usual? About something?"

Cain shrugged. "Not that I know of."

Chloe sighed, shaking her head. She might have had better luck setting up the Ways after all. "Right. Of course not."

"That wasn't what you wanted to hear," Cain observed. "Well, don't take your anger out on any of the vampires. I wouldn't care, but Ducante has some pretty strict rules. The last thing you want is to be on old man Ducante's bad side."

"He's not even here," she said grumpily.

Cain shrugged. "Well, it must be a blue moon, then. He never misses a Saturday night." He smiled. "It was nice to meet you . . ."

"Chloe," she said tersely.

"Chloe, then," he stepped forward and pushed the door open. "Stay safe."

She followed him out without saying anything. Their reemergence went unnoticed; a large group of women wearing bachelorette party sashes were creating quite a ruckus, loudly ordering drinks—overwhelming the already busy bar staff—and attracting a great deal of attention, especially since the bride-to-be was having a hard time staying upright.

For a moment, she wished she was hunting again: that group of humans would be easy pickings for vampires. And most of the vampires who'd go after them probably deserved a knife. But she didn't want to be put on Ducante's black list, so she kept her blade safely tucked away as she shuffled to the exit.

She felt frustrated as she meandered away from the bar. At

herself, for chasing her tail around a problem she only half understood. At her family, for not sharing more with her. At Sam, for misleading her. She turned a corner sharply and heard it: a voice coming from the dark alley to her left.

"Well, hello, Princess."

She tensed. A burst of energy was all she'd need and her knife would be in her hand. She turned slowly, squinting into the darkness.

"Josef," she said.

He grinned and beckoned her forward. His teeth glinted eerily in the light from the street lamps.

She stepped forward cautiously.

He wasn't wearing the dark leather jacket that had haunted her for weeks. Instead, he'd donned a black, button-up shirt under a gray tie, and fastened a black vest over both. He wore slim-fitting dress pants to match, and his shoes shone in the limited light of the alley. "Well, well, Miss Chloe. I was hoping I might see you again. Have you found any of your puzzle pieces?"

She sighed, raising her eyebrows in exasperation. "What? You mean about Pan and—"

"Shh!" he interrupted, holding up a finger in warning

"What, are you afraid they're listening?" she said tiredly. And then, snapping to attention, "Or . . . or the person who's bringing them back? Are they nearby?"

"Nonsense, Chloe. But you never know who might be channeling a long dead demon these days, do you?" He smiled again.

"Why are you lurking in an alley?" she asked suspiciously, crossing her arms over her chest.

"Waiting for some pieces to fall into place. By tomorrow, the puzzle might not be necessary at all," he said serenely.

She groaned. "Are you always so cryptic?"

"Are you always so beautiful?" he countered, taking a step toward her. "You changed your hair. It's lovely."

She rolled her eyes and turned to leave in lieu of a response.

Josef reached out to grab her arm. She felt the familiar shiver run up her spine at the chill of his touch.

"Come on, now," he said softly, pulling her back around. "I'll play nice." Slowly, he reached up, brushing a curl away from her face. A shiver that had nothing to do with his body temperature coursed through her.

She jerked away from him. "I'm not going to be your next meal, you know."

"Chloe, come now, I would *never*," he said, feigning a hurt expression. "I already ate, anyway. A lovely blonde girl. Though I'm sure she has nothing on you." He winked. Chloe was about to leave again when he said, "Whoa, hey. Sorry. What brings you here tonight?"

She shrugged. "Hitting dead ends at Ducante's."

Josef smirked. "You were trying to get information at Ducante's?" When she nodded, he chuckled. "Chloe, Chloe. The only person at Ducante's who knows anything about anything is Ducante himself, and I know he's not at that particular location tonight."

"I heard he never misses a Saturday," she challenged, hoping Cain's information was solid.

"Well, he chose to sit tonight out." He shrugged. "And so should you. Seriously. Don't let the fact that you've done nothing productive ruin your weekend."

"Well, when you put it that way," she said dryly.

"Sorry," he said, but only half-heartedly. "Look, I think my work here is just about done . . ."

"You haven't *done* anything but stand here!" she protested.

He shook his head. "It's quite rude to interrupt. Especially when I was about to invite you to a more exciting venue."

"Why?" Chloe asked, narrowing her eyes suspiciously.

Josef's widened with mock innocence. "Why, to give me the pleasure of your company, of course. And because, I think you might find you can enjoy yourself with," he dropped his voice to a faux-whisper, "a vampire."

She paused, considering. If she was perfectly honest, she had nothing better to do and no realistic hopes for productivity. But she still wasn't sure she wanted to spend the rest of her night with Josef. Or any other vampire, for that matter. "Where would we be going?"

"Oh, here and there," he replied.

"Well . . ." she began hesitantly.

As soon as the reply was out of her mouth, Josef was standing at the curbside, his arm twined through hers. "What will it take, my dear Chloe, to get you to say yes?"

On instinct, she jerked away, whipping her arm out of his reach. Casual touches were one thing—but full contact? "I . . . sorry, I don't—"

Josef waved one hand to banish her stuttered comment, shaking his head from side to side. For a moment, she thought she saw a flicker of something genuine on his face. Sadness, maybe. But in an instant, it was gone, replaced by the same toothy smile she'd come to expect.

"So what's say we get to know each other?" This time, when he reached for her, it was only to place a hand on the small of her back, guiding her gently down the sidewalk in the direction she'd originally been heading: away from the bar.

The light touch and lack of skin-to-skin contact made it more manageable. "All right," Chloe said, her composure returning. "First, tell me: who are you?"

"You know the answer to that: I'm Josef, concerned citizen and your companion for the evening."

The last line sent her stomach into a somersault. "How long has that been your identity?"

Josef's smile wavered. "A while."

"Uh-huh," she said. It was not uncommon for vampires to change identities over the course of their lifetime: it helped to blend in as the decades passed, but it also helped to cover up any villainous activities. "And what do you do that you spend your days following other people around? Who hires you to do that?"

This time she was sure she saw it: a flash of real emotion. Frustration, lingering sadness. He sighed, bowing his head as they walked. "I thought we were past this. My suggestion was that we get to know each other. Don't you want to know anything else? Like what kind of music I listen to?"

Chloe had never considered that vampires might have interests outside of predatory conquests. It was like a child trying to think of their parents as once being young—strange and disconcerting. "I . . . I don't know if that's important."

"Well, that's a very rude thing to say." He gave another sigh, this time louder and more dramatic. "What would you consider *important*?"

Why you've been following me. Who you work for. What you know, she thought blandly. What else mattered?

He rolled his eyes, holding his palms up to the sky in a defeated gesture. "Your social skills are appalling. What do you talk to your friends about?"

She heaved her shoulders in a shrug. What did she talk to her friends about? Outside of her family . . . well, who were her friends? "I don't know."

Josef made a small tsk-tsk noise. "Well, in case you *were* curious, I very much like The Doors of late." He winked. "Now you know something about me, and it's my turn for you: what do you do for fun?"

This, like so many things that came from his mouth, gave her pause. Hunting had been fun, maybe—the adrenaline of it had been invigorating. But other than that? The last thing she'd done for "fun" was a ruse, an ice cream parlor with a girl and a vampire who knew nothing of her true self.

"I thought so," he continued in a horribly self-satisfied tone. "So you have no reason to object to joining me tonight."

In an instant, he'd grabbed her arm, pulling her to the curb as he hailed a cab.

TEN

C ar rides made her nervous. She always expected them to fail or react badly to her presence. As they crossed to the west side of town, she sat, tensely gripping the handle on the taxi door, waiting for it to lurch to an unintended stop.

Josef managed a pleasant banter with the driver. It was nice; she even found herself enjoying the little quips and casual conversation. By the time they'd reached their destination, she'd almost completely forgotten she was out with a vampire.

Almost.

The club they pulled up to had, like much of the buildings on the west side of town, been an old warehouse. Trendy looking cafés sporting Shut signs dotted the area around it, along with a few buildings that had been converted into condos and apartments.

A large sign outside the club declared its name—Osin. Beneath that, a board displayed the text:

TONIGHT-CUCKOOS NEST PERFORMING.

"Is that the band you brought me here for?" Chloe asked, pointing to the sign as they climbed out of the car.

"It sure is," Josef grinned. "I think you'll find them *very* intriguing."

He led the way to the door, where he gave his name to the bouncer. The man checked the list on his clipboard and nodded them through.

The inside was a surprise, mostly because it was much more interesting than the outside. Money had clearly been pumped into remaking the interior. Large chandeliers hung at random intervals. The acrylic countertops of the bars glowed softly. And all around them, nothing but humans.

"This bar," she said, leaning close to Josef. The band hadn't started playing yet, but there was a song pumping through the speakers that made the place almost as noisy as Ducante's. "It's . . . are there any . . . ?"

"It's predominantly human, yes," he responded.

"Why did we come here?" she asked more loudly.

"To see the show, Princess!" Josef answered with a grin. He grabbed her hand and pulled her through the crowd of drunk, dancing people to a set of stairs.

At the top, another bouncer stood with a second clipboard. Josef gave his name again and the bouncer nodded, unclipping a velvet rope to let them in.

"It looks like you're pretty important here," Chloe muttered.

Josef's grin seemed permanent as he shooed her into the VIP area. "Only tonight."

The upper level was much less populated than the lower, which had almost been shoulder to shoulder. A few small loveseats with low cocktail tables were scattered throughout, and a large, circular couch dominated the area. It was clearly prime seating, looking over a railing to the raised stage on the first floor. Just like downstairs, the patrons were entirely human—except for the three women occupying the couch.

They were talking excitedly while they swayed to the music. Even though the movements were fairly basic, Chloe could instantly pinpoint them as vampires: they were too fluid, too quick. They were also dressed in especially loud clothes, even for a club setting.

One had short, blonde hair cut in a precise, asymmetrical bob. The streaks of purple running through it matched her sparkling tutu. Another had a pixie cut dyed fire-engine red, which clashed horribly with her shimmering gold mini-dress and hot pink belt. The third seemed more subdued, with black, straight hair and blunt-cut bangs. Her outfit, Chloe realized, was made entirely of lace.

As Josef led her into the VIP area, the girl with the blonde and purple bob let out a squeal of delight.

"*Josef*!" She clapped her hands together excitedly, bounding to her feet.

"You *know* them?" Chloe hissed as they approached.

Josef looked at her, bemused. "Of course. *They're* the band," he explained before the blonde girl hurtled into his torso, wrapping him in a hug. Chloe wasn't sure she'd ever seen two vampires hug. It was slightly unnerving; she was sure the force behind it was enough to break bones.

"I'm so glad you made it!" the girl gushed, pulling Josef to the couch where the other two sat. Chloe followed meekly. She could play most situations off the cuff; but a vampire taking her to meet a vampire band playing in a human bar was, like so many things this night, not a sight she'd ever expected to see.

"I am, too," he said with a warm smile. He reached out and tugged Chloe forward, nodding to the women on the couch. "This is Tashia," the blonde, "Sashia," the redhead, "and Trish," he said, acknowledging the dark-haired girl, who'd remained quiet and unenthusiastic. "Ladies, this is Chloe."

Chloe tried to summon a friendly smile. "Uh, nice to meet you."

"Ooo," squealed Tashia, "You look quite delectable, but not at all Joey's type."

"She's here as my guest," Josef said in mock warning, giving Tashia a wink.

"How fun, how fun!" the blonde giggled, clapping her hands together. "Well, thank you for coming tonight. We're the Cuckoo's Nest," she added, gesturing to the other two girls on the couch.

"As in, 'One Flew Over the'," added Sashia.

Tashia gestured to the empty seats on the large, sprawling couch. "Please, sit down, sit down! They'll be over with drinks soon."

Josef took a seat across the circle, next to Tashia, leaving Chloe to sit awkwardly next to Trish. The dark-haired vampire was still staring fixedly ahead, as if she hadn't even noticed the addition of two more people.

"Oh, don't mind her," Tashia said, waving her hand absently. "Trish had some rather special abilities before she turned, mostly in the realm of influencing. As you know—or maybe you don't?—those only get stronger once you get more supernatural blood in you." She smiled. "Now she uses them to make sure we have an excited crowd before we play."

Chloe recognized the abilities: they were from a specific psychic line that had influence over people. Especially those with weak or susceptible minds. And with everyone's mind numbed by alcohol, it probably wasn't hard for Trish to channel her powers over the entire group. Though, apparently, it took quite a bit of concentration. "Oh . . . uh. Okay. But, if you're all . . . why are you playing at a human club?"

"'A show is a show, no matter where it happens,'" said Sashia. "I think Mick Jagger said that."

"We have to play these small shows if we ever want to get signed," Tashia elaborated, smoothing out her purple tutu. "It's just part of playing the game."

"But . . . if you have her," Chloe nodded to Trish, "Why not just dazzle some music producers into putting you on their label? They're probably all human, right?"

Tashia looked taken aback. Her dark, vampire eyes widened, the expression shocking through the neon-colored makeup that coated them. "That would be the same as cheating our way to the top, and we are *not* cheaters."

"Oh, I'm sorry . . . I didn't . . . I wasn't trying to say . . ." Chloe fumbled, trying to get her mouth around a response.

Luckily, Josef intervened. "You'll have to forgive Chloe. As beautiful and talented as she is, she's still wrapping her head around vampires as multi-faceted beings that behave just like anyone else, humanity and mortality aside. She's also attempting to rediscover her social life." He ended with an infuriating wink that sent the girls into peals of laughter—or it sent Tashia into peals of laughter. Sashia simply chuckled a little. Trish had absolutely no response.

A member of the club's waitstaff finally made his way over. Josef accepted a bottle and several glasses from him, deftly filling one with an effervescent liquid before sliding it across the low table to Chloe. He was beginning to do the same to another glass, presumably for himself, when Tashia launched back into conversation.

"So, Josef. It's been *far* too long. How've you been? I don't think we've spoken since Vegas, a decade ago," she said, crossing her arms and almost pouting.

"I'm sorry," he said seriously, "I've been especially busy lately. Here, there . . ."

"Meeting new *girls*," Tashia said pointedly, her gaze sliding over to Chloe. "She's much too pretty for you, Joey."

"Sadly, I think she knows it, too," he said in a mock undertone, sending a smirk Chloe's way. "No, Tashia, Chloe and I are simply . . . business associates."

"'There's no business like show business,'" Sashia suggested. "That was in a musical."

Chloe shot her a curious look.

"Business, hm? Well, if that's what you want to talk about, how is Gavin doing?" Tashia's smirk seemed especially devilish.

Josef shifted uncomfortably. Clearly, she'd pressed a button, and clearly, she knew exactly what effect it would have. "The same as ever," he said evasively.

"So, frustrated, throwing fits, beating the help?" Tashia said with a giggle.

Josef shrugged in response.

Chloe frowned. "Who's Gavin?"

"Josef's employer," answered a soft voice next to her. Trish had come out of her reverie.

"Welcome back, Trish," Josef said good-naturedly.

"Hello, Josef. It's been too long," she replied absently. Even focused, Trish seemed a million miles away. She smiled serenely down at the stage. "We have about ten minutes before we go on."

"Bollocks," said Tashia, pouting for real. "We never get enough time together, Josef."

He shrugged. "I think you like it better that way. You can't tie down a star, after all."

"Who said that?" Sashia asked.

"The show should be quite good tonight," Trish said vaguely to no one in particular.

Tashia rolled her eyes. "It's good *every* night. Josef, darling, will I be seeing you after our performance?"

Again, a shrug. "I'm not sure. I promised Chloe a safe and relaxing evening."

The blonde grinned toothily, her gaze darting over to Chloe. "What's the fun in that?"

Chloe tried to smile. The group as a whole was hard to follow; she could barely keep track of what was said, much less dissect it for any other meaning. She covered by taking a deep sip from her glass.

The trio of women got to their feet, brushing off their outfits, smoothing their hair. They lingered a few moments longer before finally turning to exit the VIP area.

"Break a leg," Josef offered.

"Shakespeare said that," Sashia said as they disappeared down a second set of stairs near the side bar. Chloe assumed it led to the stage area.

Josef scooted over to fill the empty void between them, reaching forward to retrieve the bottle. The dark glass twinkled merrily in the lights of the club, soft peach bubbles fizzing behind the French label. He tipped a sizeable measure into Chloe's glass and shot her a sidelong grin. "Well? What did you think of them?"

She took a long sip before she responded. "They were . . . very . . . interesting."

Josef chuckled, kicking his feet up on the cocktail table and casually swinging his arm over the back of the couch. "To say the least. They've been performing for decades; you have to admire them for following their dreams."

"Always in human clubs?"

"Wherever will have them. As Sashia and Mick Jagger said," his lips twitched into another smirk, "'A show is a show.'"

Chloe shook her head and opted for another long swig of drink. "Tashia seemed to like you."

Josef laughed. "Are you jealous, Princess?"

When all she could do was stammer and blush—she wasn't sure why she'd felt the need to bring it up—he laughed harder.

"No, no. Tashia and I have a very platonic relationship. I just happened to be around when she was first turned, helped her channel her new energy into something useful."

"Do a lot of vampires join bands?" she asked, watching as a sound tech adjusted the equipment on stage. It wasn't a question she'd ever imagined asking, much less waiting patiently for an answer to, but she was thankful for the topic switch.

"A few," Josef shrugged. "What do you think we do with our time?"

It was a valid question, and one she'd never truly thought about. It filled her with the same fuzzy unease she'd felt when Josef mentioned a favorite band. Her interactions with vampires had mostly consisted of hunting them down at night, when they were searching for a meal. But she supposed they couldn't always be hunting. She'd just never bothered to think about what filled the rest of their days and nights, and finally admitted as much to Josef.

"We're not much different from how we were as humans," he said gently. "Some of us just lose our way."

She shifted uncomfortably. The memory of her last hunt sparked to life. The vampire screaming over his fallen love. The rage he'd directed at her. "Can . . . can vampires . . . you know . . . love?"

"Why?" he asked, dipping his face down so it was very close to hers. She could feel his cool breath against her skin when he spoke. "Are you looking for romance?"

"Ugh," she groaned, shifting away from him. "No, it's just . . . never mind."

"Remorse for past crimes?" he guessed, his tone more somber than it'd been a moment ago. He leaned forward, refilling her drink again. "Yes, I suppose we can love. We're not monsters, you know. At least, not exclusively."

"I've seen plenty who deserved a knife," she said harshly.

He looked at her, his expression a mixture of defensive retaliation and that indefinable emotion again. "There are plenty of humans who turn into serial killers. Shifters, even witches, go rogue on occasion. Vampires just get the most attention because of our unfortunate diets."

Chloe paused to take a drink. "You could live on animals if you wanted to."

"And I'm sure we'd still get flack for that," he sighed, settling into the couch cushions, his flash of bitter anger gone as quickly as it had appeared, hidden behind a handsome smile. "Look, Princess, let's not waste the rest of a lovely evening arguing, okay?"

She shrugged, but wasn't entirely sure she was ready to comply. "So . . . this person . . ." *What had his name been?* ". . . that you work for?"

"That's a story for another time," he interrupted, pointing to the stage. Tashia, Sashia, and Trish were taking their places: Tashia marched up to the lead microphone, Sashia had a guitar strapped around her torso, and Trish was off to the side with a keyboard.

Tashia's lips were all but pressed to the microphone as she introduced the band, "We're Cuckoo's Nest, ladies and gentlemen!"

"As in 'One Flew Over the'," added Sashia. The crowd cheered wildly as the thrum of their first song rang out over the speakers.

"They're not half bad," Chloe said, her words slurring. The ice of alarm slipped down her back. How many drinks had she had? She set her glass down, trying to remember. The music sounded distorted, as if she were hearing it through static. Her heart was beating quickly—too quickly—and everything about her was so *heavy*.

"No, they're not," he shouted, clapping his hands and whooping as a particularly loud, electronic-synth melody took over after Sashia's guitar solo.

"Josef, I . . ." she licked her lips. Why was it taking so long to make a sentence? She shook her head and then looked at him: two Josef's swam in her vision.

They looked at her with expressions somewhere between apologetic and triumphant, but that was as much as she could gather. Her eyelids drooped, carrying her into the twilight between waking and sleeping.

"Whoa, whoa, whoa . . ." she heard him say through layers of water. She felt him lean her gently back on the couch—had she tipped forward? It was hard to tell. All her senses felt disconnected; she couldn't even be sure she still had a body. The music and lights of the club barely seemed to exist, swimming in a distorted sort of harmony through her mind.

Dimly, she was aware of another figure coming to sit on the couch next to the phantom, second Josef. There was something familiar about the figure's gray-streaked hair, but her mind was foggy, heavy. She couldn't place it and she didn't care to try.

"Is it taken care of?"

She'd heard that voice before . . .

"I watched her leave the bar myself, just before coming here. She wouldn't leave unless the job was done."

No, no, she knew *this* voice.

Josef, she thought, clinging to the name as a way back to the world.

"This could ruin my reputation, you know. But I suppose if it stops . . . Well, it's all for the better." A sigh. "You really went out of your way to keep this one from being involved."

"She didn't need to be. *Doesn't* need to be."

The other voice snorted. "It's all she's *meant* to be. Surely you understand her kind by now. You must really care about her, bringing her here."

"Whatever," snapped Josef. "Bring the car around so we can get out of this hell-hole."

"Hell-hole?" the second voice sounded offended. "This bar is one of my particular favorites."

And then it was too much. She felt her senses breaking away. Strong, cold hands lifted her off the couch as her mind let go and she fell into true oblivion.

ELEVEN

"**M**ikhail?" she breathed into the gloom. Rain pounded against the roof. Lightning cracked outside, illuminating the darkness.

Her brother stood at the window, his back to her, his hands clutching the windowsill. He was dripping wet, his hair plastered to his skull. His shirt and pants were dark from the rain, as if he'd run out in it suddenly.

"Mikhail!" she cried.

Something was wrong; something had to be wrong. She ran into the room, her favorite quilt clutched to her chest.

He turned to face her, tears mingling with the rainwater on his face. She tripped on the fabric's corner, sprawling on the ground.

He didn't have to say it. She knew her parents were gone. There was a void in the house, an emptiness where there should have been warmth, comfort.

The puddle at her brother's feet reflected sharply as lightning pierced the shadows.

The rain.

Mikhail had been in the rain . . . her parents could be out there.

Before the thought was fully formed, she was out the door, the quilt forgotten.

She paused, peering through the darkness as the ocean wind slammed against her. Wiping the water and tears from her vision, she sprinted for the stone steps that led to the sand and water. They'd be down there. They *had* to be.

The stone was slick; only her partially emerged powers kept her upright. She slid on the edge of a step, tripping down several more before catching her balance. Dimly, she could hear the slap of Mikhail's feet as he came tearing after her.

Waves crashed angrily against the empty stretch of sand as lightning ripped across the sky, tearing through the clouds.

She stumbled. Cold grit clung to the soles of her feet as she ran toward the water.

"Momma!" she shrieked, her voice cracking with desperation. Fear and pain swelled until it tore out in a wordless scream. Howling, she threw herself into the rain-tossed surf, the water rushing in to crush her. She coughed and sputtered as the cold liquid filled her mouth, choking off her screams.

And then Mikhail was there. Wrapping his arms around her, he pulled her from the waves. She coughed. She wanted to struggle—against him, against the world, against all of it—but her body was so *heavy*.

Mikhail's form shivered, morphing into Josef. Her limbs transformed from chubby childhood to lithe adult and she was suddenly acutely aware that none of it was real. She was dreaming. She *had* to be dreaming.

"Chloe," the voice belonged to neither, a mix of Mikhail's rough tones and Josef's smooth ones. "Chloe!"

The waves were behind them. They were trudging up the stone steps, slower than necessary. By the time they reached the house, she was cold, confused: was this memory? Dream? Or was this happening?

Where was she?

Her head swam as the still-shifting figure of Mikhail/Josef laid her down on the pink sheets of her childhood bed.

"I'm sorry, Chloe," said the strange, blended voice. "I hope you'll forgive me one day."

That wasn't what happened . . . , she thought in vague response. The figure faded to nothing and she was alone in the rapidly darkening room.

The darkness scared her more than it should have. Something felt distinctly wrong. She tried to bury herself in the blankets, but the feeling didn't subside.

She heard scratching, knocking, banging noises coming from somewhere nearby and opened her mouth to scream . . .

è

Chloe's eyes shot open. Her mind raced through a dozen horrible scenarios before she became conscious of the fact she was in her own home, once again on the overstuffed couch.

At some point, a blanket had been placed over her, but she'd flung it across the room. It lay in a crumpled pile, uncomfortably similar to the forgotten quilt in her dream.

What happened last night? Slowly, she retraced her steps: Ducante's. Leaving Ducante's. Running into . . . running into Josef. The last thing she could recall was his face swimming out of focus. She gritted her teeth angrily, tightening her fists around a pillow.

He was responsible for the near coma she'd just come out of. He had to be. But why? A quick inspection revealed she was uninjured. Her jacket had been removed and laid neatly on the table, her knife still holstered in its sleeve.

She didn't feel light-headed, hadn't been fed on. But her mouth felt paper-dry, and there was a slight tremor in her limbs from the horrible memory-turned-nightmare. The images were starting to fade, but she could still hear the scratching and knocking.

Tap, tap, tap.

Chloe froze, all the hair on her body standing on end. That had *not* been her imagination. It came from her front door.

When she got to her feet, her legs were shaking. Her hands felt thick and dumb as she attempted to shake the knife out of her jacket.

By the time she wobbled to the door, the tapping had faded to a vague scratching. Her mind felt clouded, foggy; no rational excuse for the noise came to her. She took a deep breath, trying to steady herself, and wrenched the door open.

Initially, she saw nothing. Just her yard, the trees.

A choked sound drew her eyes to the pale, dark-haired boy curled up on her doorstep.

Sam.

"What . . . why . . . ?" she began, feeling utterly bewildered. At her voice, he turned his head toward her.

Chloe gasped. His skin, always so pale, was even whiter than usual. Ghostly. In some places, it was almost transparent. Dark circles rimmed his eyes, which were bloodshot in a way she'd never seen on a vampire.

"Ch . . . Chlo . . ." he choked, reaching weakly toward her legs.

"Damn," she whispered. "What happened to you?"

He tried to sputter a response, but it was quickly drowned in a groan of pain.

"Sam?" she asked tentatively. "I'm going to try to get you inside, okay?"

He gave a miniscule nod. She knelt down, grabbed him under the arms and heaved him across the threshold.

He screamed in earnest, a bone-chilling cry of pain.

She was stronger than a human would be, but she still felt a nervous sweat break across her brow. His body was dead weight. She managed to get him just inside the door before she gave up. "Sam. Sam, hold on, okay? I'm going to get some stuff."

A weak groan was her only reply. She didn't bother to click the door shut, taking off toward the living room instead. She snatched up a pillow, the discarded blanket, and paused. What good would that do an ailing vampire?

She cursed and dashed over to a bookshelf. She wasn't a healer. But her parents, they'd been able to heal just about anything. She scanned the titles quickly, looking for something medical related. There weren't any. Of course. They'd never kept books on the subject—they already knew all they needed. They'd never passed it down, though, and now she had no help.

"Sam?" she said as she returned, kneeling next to him. "I brought you some stuff to make you more comfortable. I'm going to try and help you, but you have to tell me what happened, okay?"

Sam grimaced. His eyes were scrunched shut, his fangs bared. He didn't say anything as she eased the pillow behind his head.

"Look, I'm not asking this for fun," she said again, trying to keep the panic from her voice. "If you don't tell me, I literally can't do a thing for you."

It was one of the caveats of the Naimei ability. Their magic was filled with checks and balances, most profoundly in healing. The body was so complex, the healer either had to be told what was wrong or witness the injury themselves if they had any chance of fixing it. Going in blind created an unstable magic that could be deadly to both parties.

"Last . . ." Sam licked his lips, pausing as he tried to gather himself. His hands clenched tightly around the edges of the blanket. "Blood . . . bad."

"Keep talking, Sam, I need more than that." She brushed her hair back and rubbed her hands together, trying to remember how to do a full-body healing.

"B-blood . . . p-p-poison . . ." a shudder went through him, followed by a pained shout.

"Whoa, whoa, okay!" she said quickly. "Easy, you did great . . . easy. Okay . . . here we go . . ."

As carefully as possible, she set her hands in place: one on his head, one on his heart. Sam cringed. Chloe squeezed her eyes shut, trying to focus on his body. At first, nothing seemed to happen. She took a deep, shaking breath; as she exhaled, she felt some of her power slip through her fingertips into Sam's shaking form.

Suddenly, it was as if she existed in two places at once, like she could see inside him without seeing at all.

She tried desperately to sort through what was normal, what was healthy. The majority of his body felt dead beneath the soft thrum of her magic, but was that how vampires were supposed to feel? The limited healing she'd done had certainly never been on the undead.

Sam let out a hiss of pain as she dug deeper, but it was distant now. She barely noticed. She almost had a baseline established, and could feel that something was definitely, horribly wrong. If she could just find it, she could draw it out, fix it.

"What the *hell* are you doing?" said a harsh voice from miles away.

Chloe jerked to attention. Her power pulled sharply from Sam's core—he howled in pain. In the doorway, Rus's form swam into view. His arms were laden with more dusty, leatherbound volumes, his jaw open in shock.

"Why the hell is there a dying vampire on your floor?"

For a moment, she mouthed wordlessly at him. "I . . . he's not . . . something happened, but . . . well, I can help, and—"

"Do you have any idea how dangerous this is?" His tone sounded much less like the calm, docile one she'd come to expect, and much more like . . . well, Alex. "Just because you're not hunting them anymore doesn't mean you have to go out of your way to save them, Chloe."

"Rus, something's really wrong, and I can—"

"This is not what you were instructed to do. If we wanted you to play with vampires, we wouldn't have asked you to do anything different!" he snapped, throwing the books to the ground with a heavy thud. "Doesn't it matter to you that the entire balance of the world is in jeopardy?"

"Yes, but—"

"Have you even attempted to practice the Ways? To find out anything about that human you're following?"

"Rus—"

"This selfish behavior is why you're not trusted with bigger responsibilities, because clearly you can't—"

"Rus!" Chloe said sharply. Her exclamation came with a well-timed moan from Sam, who looked even worse than he had when he'd first arrived. "This isn't right. It's not natural. We can fix this, right here, right now, without any guesswork." She took a deep breath. "Either help me or don't, but I'm not going to watch him die in my living room."

For a heartbeat, Rus simply glowered. Then he sank down, kneeling across from her, Sam's broken body between them. "Guide me and I'll help you."

She took a deep breath. "Thank you," she whispered as she again placed her hands: one on Sam's head, one on his heart. "It's some type of poisoning, by the way, from bad blood."

Rus didn't say anything, but pressed his hands firmly over her's.

She felt Rus's power before she felt her own. His was stronger, steadier: it shoved its way through her hands, pulling her magic with it as it dived into Sam's frail body. She knew what to do this time, where to go; she sifted through organs, tissues, the remnants of whatever blood he'd ingested the night before.

She could feel it; tiny bits of matter, tiny daggers, tearing into everything within Sam. It was the nature of a vampire to regenerate. But this poison was too aggressive. Sam's body couldn't keep up. It was grinding him down too quickly.

Her magic pointed the way to the foul presence. She felt Rus nod in agreement. All it took was one focused push—she could dimly hear Rus muttering the words to a spell—and the magic began drawing the toxin out. Sam convulsed wildly beneath her hands. She pressed down firmly to keep from losing the connection.

In an instant, it was over. Chloe felt her powers retract, pulling her back into her own body. She locked eyes with Rus as he removed his hands from hers and sat back. She followed suit, her gaze drifting to Sam. His chest bore two candy-apple red marks.

Her palms felt sticky. She turned them over cautiously; they were coated with a vaguely-purple, rancid smelling substance.

"Blech!" she exclaimed, wiping her hands on the blanket. "What the hell is that?"

Rus frowned, tugging the blanket toward him. He sniffed at the substance, eyeing it skeptically. After a moment of observation, he slipped a knife from his pocket and cut the tainted piece out, folding it carefully before returning both to his pocket. "It's curious, that's what it is."

Chloe's eyes fell on Sam. He was still motionless. The handprints were fading very, very slowly, but his eyes were still shut. "Is . . . is he . . . ?"

Rus sighed and reached across the vampire's body. He seized her hand and placed it once again over the boy's heart. "Check for yourself. You have to feel deep . . . there. Do you feel it?"

There was no heartbeat or breath sounds, but there was *something*; a distant thrum of life. She let out a sigh of relief. Her own heart was slamming in her chest from the effort of healing.

Rus shook his head and relaxed back onto his heels. "Why do you get yourself into these situations, Chloe?"

"Hey, it's not my fault," she began defensively. "He came to me."

"Then why are sickly vampires showing up on your doorstep?" he challenged.

She bit her lip. "I . . . he . . . I was doing that other thing Alex asked. You know . . . keeping my ears open. Looking for information."

Rus arched his eyebrows. "Oh? And this guy is who you found? Did he have anything useful to say?"

"Well . . ." Chloe sighed. Saying much more would dig her into a deeper hole of trouble. As mad as she was at Josef, she was still unwilling to share his existence with her family. How would they react? Especially to what had happened the night before? "Sort of. Not really. He said people were nervous, but . . . but it was all just dead ends."

Her cousin shook his head again. "People are always nervous, Chloe."

"I know that *now*," she said stubbornly, crossing her arms over her chest.

"Look," Rus started, running a hand through his hair. "This situation is serious. I know you're just trying to be involved, but Alex would have told you more if he thought you were ready to hear it. The person we're looking for is elusive; the Ways can't get a clear read on them."

"So it doesn't matter that I haven't been using them. They wouldn't have helped anyway," Chloe interjected.

Rus frowned, and she went silent. "We think he's cloaking himself with the powers of other supernaturals; too many to even say what kind. It's nothing we've seen before, and we aren't getting very far. The only lead we have," he fixed her with a stern gaze, "is the girl you're tailing."

Chloe felt his unspoken disappointment settle over her like an invisible weight. It made her feel sick to her stomach.

"Have you found out anything about her?" he added gently. His tone suggested that he already anticipated the answer to be no.

"I spent all day yesterday researching," Chloe offered softly. "I . . . she didn't match any of the lines. Her powers have only manifested once, and I haven't seen anything since. She's aware that when they come out something strange happens, but she doesn't know what. And she certainly can't control it."

Rus nodded, listening quietly. "Well, then you need to try and force them out of her. What she can do—the reason she's involved in all of this—might be the only other clue we get on how to find this vampire."

She bit her lip and gave a slow nod.

Her cousin glanced down at Sam's motionless form. He stood silently and walked out the door. Chloe stared after him, bewildered, until he reappeared a few moments later with something in his hand.

"He'll need to feed," he said dully, tossing her a plastic container.

She caught it with a shiver. A blood bag, no doubt lifted from a local hospital.

"Is there anything else you want to tell me?" Rus asked, leaning against the doorframe, his arms crossed over his chest.

There's a vampire who definitely knows what's going on. But don't worry, he seems harmless; or, at least, he did until he drugged me at a human club last night, was what she should have said. But instead, she simply shrugged.

"I expected more out of you, Chloe," he said placidly, turning to leave.

"Rus?" she said tentatively. He looked back over his shoulder, and she quickly added, "I'm . . . I'm sorry. And . . . thank you."

It was his turn to shrug before he vanished into thin air. She stared at the spot for a solid minute before realizing she'd never asked why he'd come by in the first place.

෴

It took awhile to rouse Sam enough to give him the blood. He was practically comatose—shaking him and yelling only caused his brow to furrow. She rocked back on her heels, frowning. It made sense that, in his weakened state, he'd be more likely to sleep during the day, but this was ridiculous. Night was several hours off, and she didn't have time to play host to a pseudo-corpse.

She retrieved the knife she'd dropped when she saw Sam crumpled at her door and used it to open the tube on the blood bag. She waved it under his nose, hoping the smell would entice him into consciousness.

Sam twitched once or twice before his eyes opened; his hands snatched the bag quicker than she could follow. As his lips closed over the open tube, she felt her stomach somersault; it was sickly reminiscent of a human child with a juice box.

As he tried to extract the final drops from the plastic, she broke the silence. "So . . . you're feeling better, then."

He frowned, but nodded ever so slightly.

"Yeah. Yeah, I am," he said, looking down and flexing his hands experimentally. "Look, Chloe . . ."

"Don't worry about it," she said, waving her hand in the air. "After hunting for so long, the least I could do—"

"I don't like owing people favors," he said bluntly.

"Oh," she finished. It hadn't been gratitude coming her way, after all.

He sighed, running his hand through his hair and tilting his head to the side as he looked at her. "You're different from other witches."

She shrugged in response. "Is that why you came to me?"

He set the plastic container down, gazing into the living room at the disheveled couch. "I thought I was dying."

"You *were* dying," she confirmed.

Sam looked at her, his expression hard and unreadable. "I'm sorry about the way I've acted around you. You're hard to get a read on."

"Oh, I'm just all over the map," she said blandly, plucking at the loose threads Rus had created in her blanket.

"Look, what I'm trying to say is . . . I . . . well." He sighed. "Whatever. I owe you."

"Sure, okay," Chloe said with an eye roll. "*Thanks*, Sam. Are you going to be okay?"

"Yeah," he replied, trying to get to his feet. He was about halfway there when he stumbled, still unsteady on his legs.

Chloe stood quickly, holding out a hand to steady him. "Whoa, whoa."

He caught her hand the same time he caught his balance. If vampires could blush, she was sure he would have been bright red. He let go of her hand and walked hurriedly toward the door. He mumbled something about taking care as he reached the front step.

"Hey, wait! What happened to you last night?" Chloe called after his retreating form.

He turned back to look at her, a snarl on his face. "Some shifter-witch turned hunter. Can you believe it? At *Ducante's.*

That place is going to the dogs." He shook his head. "Whatever. See you around, Witch," he added before taking off, fast as ever, toward the tree line.

Chloe ran a hand through her hair as she gazed at the mess her small house had become. Her head had been foggy from whatever Josef had slipped her when she'd started healing, but now, a definite, throbbing pain was growing in her temples. She had no time for that, though.

Sam wasn't the only one who needed to have a word with a certain bar owner.

TWELVE

B etween sips of water and bites of food, she scrubbed at the dark makeup still caked on her face. Her stomach was boiling, but she forced the sustenance down anyway, knowing it would ebb her headache and fix the shaking that hadn't stopped since she'd awakened. It would do nothing for the sore muscles cropping up all over her body, but she ignored that as she showered and dressed. She had more important matters to deal with, like her quickly waning patience.

She couldn't stand the thought of walking, running, or even driving to her destination; they'd all take far too long. So, despite the stiffness she felt spreading through her shoulders, she pulled herself into the nothingness of space as soon as she was beyond her front door.

When she reappeared, she was standing in the same alley she'd met Josef in the night before. She half expected to see him standing there, a would-be-charming grin plastered on his face, some cryptic message ready on his lips. It certainly would have shortened her search, but instead, she found herself quite alone.

She wasn't sure what she'd do if Ducante was away from his bar for a second night. Taking hostages was usually counter-productive to balancing the universe, but if she was already operating off the map, what could it hurt?

She shoved her way through the front door of Ducante's, glad to see Ducante himself standing behind the bar, no other staff in sight. He looked slightly bored; his gray-streaked head was bent toward a pile of papers while he lazily polished a group of silver-rimmed glasses. He looked up as she entered, a sly grin spreading across his features.

"Well, if it isn't Chloe Naimei. What brings you in at this early hour? You don't strike me as much of a daytime drinker. Not with that sweet, young face, anyway." His voice retained a slightly unctuous tone that made Chloe's fists tighten.

"Where. Is. He," she said through gritted teeth, marching to the bar.

Ducante set the glass he'd been working on down and picked up another. "My dear Chloe, you'll have to be more specific about the 'he' to which you are referring. There are many 'he's' who come in and out, including one I believe you had a rendezvous with in my supply closet just last night. I'll add those bottles you tested to your tab, by the way."

Chloe's mind whirred—who had she rendezvoused with in the supply closet . . . ? Ah, yes. Cain. Her brother's friend. Were Ducante's sources that good?

"You know *exactly* who I'm talking about. Where the hell is Josef?"

He sighed, rubbing at a particularly stubborn spot. "Well, my dear, that's a fine question. Though, last I checked, I am neither his keeper nor his maker."

"You pass messages for him" she snarled. "You know where he is."

Ducante shook his head, squinting into the glass as he held it up to the light. "Just because he occasionally makes an appearance here does not mean I'm privy to where he goes after he leaves."

Chloe bit the inside of her lip to keep from grinding her teeth. She raised two fingers, bringing them down sharply on top of the bar. The glass in Ducante's hand shattered; the shards buried themselves a quarter of an inch into the gleaming wood surface.

Ducante took a deep breath. When he looked up, his expression was harder than she'd yet seen. There were dozens of small cuts on his fingers, but they were already beginning to close.

"While I appreciate your appetite for chaos, Chloe, I'm afraid I cannot tolerate those who choose to damage my property."

She forced her voice to stay level. "You know where Josef is. And *he* knows about Pan and Damonos."

Ducante's eyes flashed their true, demonic red. He vaulted over the bar, standing within inches of her face. "What do you think you know," he said icily, "about Pan and Damonos?"

"I know they're the original demons," she said, holding her chin high to meet his gaze. "I know someone is trying to bring them back. I know that Josef knows. And I know," she said, steeling herself for the potential repercussions of her wild guesswork, "that you're probably gunning for their return."

Faster than any vampire, he grabbed her arm and spun her so that her upper back was pressed firmly against the bronze edge of the bar. She screamed as her skin exploded into angry boils. With her free hand, she unsheathed the knife at her hip and dragged it across his chest.

He released her and jumped back, hissing as he clutched at the red stain spreading across his torn shirt. "I am not one to pick a fight with, Chloe."

"Then tell me what I need to know!" she shouted, tightening her grip on the knife. "You know where Josef is. You know who's trying to bring Pan and Damonos back. You're fighting for it to happen!"

Ducante let out another low hiss. "I most certainly am *not* fighting to bring them back. Just because we share lineage does not mean I anticipate their return."

She frowned.

"Pan and Damonos are dangerous: they wouldn't hesitate to slaughter every creature on this earth, be it human, vampire, Naimei, or demon. They never evolved into organized chaos: they practice the old ways, following the lines of complete and utter madness. And as of an hour ago," Ducante prodded at the healing cut on his chest, examining the slice in his shirt, "the situation surrounding their return should have been remedied."

"That's not what our sources say," Chloe said sharply.

"Your *sources*?" Ducante snorted. "You mean your Naimei Ways? In the event you haven't learned already, that method is far from practical."

"How is yours any better?" she challenged. Her back still felt like it was on fire. She'd elected for nothing more than a tank top, so the burn stretched from shoulder to shoulder.

Ducante rolled his eyes. "My dear, are you familiar with the phrase, 'don't look a gift horse in the mouth?' I'm offering you a way out of dealing with this mess. It would be in your best interest to accept it." He sighed. "Have a seat. You're obviously close to collapsing."

"I'm—"

"I can smell your energy, girl. You don't have enough to fix that wound; you barely have enough to stand. Have a seat while I get something that'll help." He pointed sharply at the fallen bar stools and they clattered to a standing position.

Grudgingly, Chloe accepted a seat. Ducante resumed his position behind the bar, shuffling through bottles on the bottom shelf.

"I don't think I believe you. About them not being brought back anymore," she said stubbornly.

The bottles clinked as he moved them aside. "Well, then how about this: I'll believe as I do, and you'll worry as you do. And if the time comes that evidence proves me wrong, well, then, I suppose I'll join you in the panic. Ah, here we go," he said, rising with a small, green bottle.

He moved out from behind the bar. She eyed him warily. "What is that?"

"Think of it as a healing solution; a simple concoction, really. I realize it's not Naimei magic, but under the circumstances, I feel you'd prefer this to my particular brand of abilities." He pulled a cork out of the bottle and held it up to the light. "Do you mind if I . . . ?" He made a pouring motion in the direction of her shoulders. "It won't heal you outright, but it will remove the substance that causes that nasty burn. Speed up the process, you know."

Chloe shrugged. What's the worst that could happen?

He tipped the bottle onto the bright red blisters. She cried out as the liquid seared over her shoulders. "Oh. I'm sorry," he said in a faux-polite tone. "Did I not mention it would sting?"

He smiled.

She swore under her breath.

"Now, that is most unladylike. Consider us even," he added, plucking at the jagged fabric running across his chest. "Do you realize how difficult it is to come by Armani in this town?"

She shrugged, rolling her shoulders experimentally. Despite the initial sting, the solution did seem to be working; coolness was spreading where the burn had been. If it calmed the blisters, she'd be able to heal with very little effort. "You never answered my other question."

"And that would be?" he asked vaguely, returning to his preferred side of the bar as he began digging glass out of the wood.

"Josef," she said seriously, "where is he?"

Ducante paused and looked up at her. "Why do his where-abouts concern you so much? Is the princess missing her knight in shining armor?"

She gritted her teeth and chose the path of blatant honesty. "He drugged me last night. I'd like to know why."

To her great dismay, Ducante simply chuckled and went back to removing the glass shards. Thick drops of his darker-than-normal blood were falling onto the bar, but he didn't seem to notice or care. "Ah, so there's no knight for the princess after all, is there? Maybe he was angry about your storage-closet tryst."

"This isn't a joke!" she said sharply, slapping her hand on the bar. "And you know as well as I do there was no tryst. I want to know what game he's playing. I know you know more than you're letting on."

"Josef is indisposed, my dear." He pulled out the largest of the glass chunks, moving on to some of the smaller slivers. "It would benefit both of you if you let the issue drop now, rather than later."

Chloe narrowed her eyes. "This isn't the sort of issue you just drop."

"Well, I suggest you *make* it an issue you just drop." He stopped meddling with the bar and fixed her with a serious ex-pression. "Despite what your Naimei superiority might be telling you, there are more important things in the world—and certainly in Josef's life—than you. Whatever he did was obviously done with reason."

"I doubt it," she said coldly.

For a moment, he looked as if he were about to deliver a stinging retort. He opened his mouth quickly, and then shut it, closing his eyes and sucking in a deep breath. "Then, my dear, we find ourselves at an impasse." He snatched the rag he'd been polishing with and wiped some of his blood from the counter. "I'm afraid I have nothing else to offer you, and you clearly have nothing but an argument."

She stared at him warily, unsure what to say.

"So," he continued, "until you need a supernatural meeting place or a stiff drink, it's probably time you leave. There's already been enough worry about a hunter in my bar."

Chloe slid smoothly off the stool, replacing the knife in its sheath. "From what I've heard, you have a lot more to worry about than hunters. Or is a poisoned vampire a regular Saturday-night thing here?"

Ducante's eyes widened in momentary surprise before narrowing suspiciously. "What would you know about that?"

"You're not the only one with sources," she said slyly. She paused as she reached the door, turned and blew him a kiss before pushing her way out onto the street.

❧

Despite her unwillingness to agree with a demon, she couldn't deny the fact she was very near collapse. Magic was out of the question, so she walked a few blocks away and summoned a cab from the quickly darkening streets. It would take her longer than she liked to get home, but at least she'd make it in one piece.

Her biggest problem with the supernatural world was that there was no one to turn to after a particularly awful day. Injured humans could visit a hospital: they'd be treated physically, and, if the occasion called for it, mentally, as well. The most a supernatural could do was heal, if their powers allowed it, and hope for a better day tomorrow. Even if there was someone around to talk to, it was unlikely anything would be that out of the ordinary. It was just normal life on the supernatural side of things.

By the time she made it home, she felt ready to drop. The muscles that had been sore before were burning now. She barely kept herself upright long enough to stand under the stream of hot shower-water and inspect the wounds on her back. She didn't fully trust Ducante, but was pleased to see that after a short, agonizing burst of energy, the burn was gone. The skin was baby pink and new-looking, tender but healing.

She managed to pull on a t-shirt and shorts before collapsing onto her bed, grateful she'd made it there instead of spending another night on the couch. Within seconds, blessed sleep pulled her into sweet oblivion.

❧

"Whoa," Aurelia said as Chloe slumped into homeroom. "Someone had a rough weekend."

Chloe grunted in response. She hadn't been troubled by dreams, but she'd still barely felt the effects of sleep. Her muscles ached and she felt extremely weak. It had been all she could do to pull her hair into a loose braid and select an outfit that—sort of—matched. Now, all she could think was that the fluorescent lights were terribly uncomfortable.

Aurelia nodded wisely. "Out chasing the many men in your life?"

She groaned and put her head on the desk. Aurelia was too chipper: her very presence was making her feel immensely guilty. Today would be another wasted day. How was she supposed to investigate the powers of a would-be psychic when she could barely keep her head up?

School passed in a haze. She felt like a zombie as she walked from class to class—useless. In fact, the only time she felt the need to gather a complete sentence was when they reached the cafeteria.

"What the hell is *that*?" she asked scathingly, pointing at a poster on the wall.

There were two. One depicted a rather demure image of Corinne wrapped in a Herve Leger-esque sparkling dress. Flowery writing read: "Vote Corinne Degraw for Spring Fling queen!"

The other was much more plain. In nothing but bold text, it read: "Chloe Moraine for Spring Fling queen." And, in smaller letters beneath that, "A nicer option."

"That's . . . uh . . . you know. Corinne's Spring Fling campaign . . ."

"That's *not* what I'm talking about," Chloe hissed, walking over to examine the signs more closely. "Did you do this?"

"No!" Aurelia exclaimed, holding her hands up defensively. "No way. I stay out of politics."

Chloe shook her head in disbelief. "Who else knows me well enough to put up signs about me?"

The other girl shifted uncomfortably. "Well . . . uh. Roger, maybe . . . he might've told some people about what you did. You know, saving him from being merged with a locker."

"He hasn't even talked to me since that happened!"

Aurelia shrugged. "Maybe when he kept coming up to you . . . he was trying to ask permission to start a campaign."

"Damn it," Chloe said, tugging at her braid in aggravation. This was the last thing she needed. She tried to tell Aurelia as much, but her efforts were interrupted when two nervous-looking girls holding lunch trays shuffled up.

"Um, Chloe?" one of them asked tentatively. She was a tall, willowy girl with straight, blonde hair. Chloe didn't know her, but she did look vaguely familiar—they shared a class, maybe.

"We just wanted to say, um, good luck with the Spring Fling!" the second girl—short, curvy, and dark-haired—said. "You . . . um . . . you'd be really good as the queen!"

Chloe gaped as they quickly trundled off to a table. "There are people who *support this?*"

Aurelia fidgeted. "Well . . . yeah. I mean . . . just the people who aren't fans of Corinne."

"So the whole school."

"Well, not the *entire* school . . . but a strong part. For sure." She picked at a loose thread on the hem of her shirt.

"Damn it," Chloe repeated, staring at the sign. "I don't even want to go to this dance."

"Come on," Aurelia chided, grabbing Chloe's arm and guiding her toward the line for food. "You *have* to go. People are cheering for you! And it's your senior Spring Fling—you can't miss that."

She sighed. "I . . . this should be going to someone else. Someone who belongs here."

"What are you talking about?" Aurelia asked, eyeing a sandwich with great skepticism before picking it up. "Of course you belong here."

Chloe cringed. *If only she knew.* "I mean, you know, someone who's gone here for longer than a week."

"Hey," Aurelia replied as she plucked an orange juice from the counter, "a win is a win as long as it's not for Corinne. At least in my book."

"I think Mick Jagger said that," Chloe muttered, before remembering how angry she was at that entire night. When the other girl gave her a quizzical look, she shook her head. "Never mind. Let's just sit down."

Apparently, she'd been missing out on quite a lot by not sitting in the cafeteria. Slowly, a wide array of students nervously joined the table she and Aurelia had chosen. Each seemed to have something encouraging to say about her campaign for Spring Fling queen. A few even had rumors they needed confirmed or denied about what Chloe had been like at "her old school".

"Is it true you got a teacher fired for yelling at a student?" one girl asked, her voice hushed. The boy next to her elbowed her sharply in the ribs, and she shot him a scandalized look. "What? I need to know!"

Chloe denied everything, shooting horrified looks at Aurelia over the more ridiculous rumors. At the beginning of the onslaught, she'd tried to encourage people to vote for someone else; but when it became apparent that humility just made her seem more appealing, she quickly gave up.

Five minutes to the bell, she and Aurelia escaped into the hallway on the pretense of getting to class early.

"How did I end up some high school celebrity?" she grumbled. She felt more drained than ever, and her head was spinning with all the things she supposedly was. Chloe Moraine, high school superhero by day, universe balancer and occasional vampire hunter by night.

"Curse of the pretty people," Aurelia said with a shrug, slipping into the classroom.

Chloe scowled and followed.

The only good thing that could be said for the last part of the day was that it went by more quickly than the first. Due, in part, to the fact she was now aware of the subtle ways students reacted to her: the one time she was called on in Chemistry, her half-assed answer earned nods of approval from at least half the class.

By the time the final bell rang, she felt uncomfortable, confused, and utterly exhausted. Her only thought was getting home to her bed.

Aurelia turned to her with a smile. "Ready to go?"

"Uh," Chloe said, blinking in surprise. "Where?"

Aurelia frowned. "To work on the project."

"To . . . what?" Had this been one of the many things she'd absently agreed to in the morning?

"To work on the project! Come on, Chloe, just because you're popular now doesn't mean you can bail on all our work. You agreed it would be best to get the science-y part done today, and then we can do the actual baking later in the week." She stood up, shoving the last of her books into her bag.

Chloe tried, for the umpteenth time that day, to suppress a groan. "I . . . right. Sure. Your place?"

Aurelia gave a firm nod.

❧

Twenty minutes later, Chloe found herself in Aurelia's living room, rather than her own bed. Aurelia, of course, was completely unfazed by that fact. The girl managed to keep the same level of chatter she had throughout the school day, though the subject had changed from the weekend to the much more sleep-inducing topic of their science project.

She produced a number of snack-food items from the fridge before settling down among a pile of library books in the super-modern living room.

Chloe nibbled on a cracker, hoping it would keep her awake.

For an hour and a half, she searched through book after book. Aurelia seemed to have a flair for Chemistry, or, at least, she understood more than Chloe; in every book, she managed to select a chapter that gave them *something* they could cite in a report.

Around the fifth book, Chloe could feel her eyes drooping. She'd been fighting the impulse for a while, but it seemed clear the fight was in vain. She felt her head drop listlessly forward, and in an instant, she was asleep.

❧

"Mikhail!" she cried.

Something was wrong; something had to be wrong. She ran into the room, her favorite quilt clutched to her chest.

He turned to face her, tears mingling with the rainwater on his face. She tripped on the fabric's corner, sprawling on the ground.

Somehow, the space looked different. It was more vivid: the tiles pulsed with color, the windows seemed etched in stark relief against the darkness. She could hear the Ways whirring on the table that filled half the kitchen.

Confused, she stood, the quilt forgotten. A shout pierced the air, ricocheting off the walls. Chloe covered her ears and ducked . . .

❧

She jerked awake. Her face was pressed against the book she'd been reading; she sat up quickly, smoothing her hair and trying to look as if nothing happened. She didn't want to disappoint Aurelia and add another name to the list of people she'd failed.

But when she glanced up, Aurelia had a look of dazed confusion on her face. As if she, too, was just coming out of a short sleep.

Chloe opened her mouth to say something, to brush off the moment with a light-hearted comment, but Aurelia spoke first.

"Who's Mikhail?" she asked vaguely.

"My brother," Chloe answered. She couldn't remember ever mentioning his name to the other girl. "How did you . . . ?"

Aurelia's brow furrowed. She didn't say anything; her eyes darted nervously to Chloe and then to the floor. It was the same way she'd behaved that first day, when her powers had cracked through the surface.

"Did I . . . was I talking in my sleep?" Chloe offered gently.

"Oh. Uh . . . yeah. Yeah, I think you said the name once or twice," Aurelia replied. "Look, uh, I'm sorry. I didn't realize you were that tired. We can call it a night."

"Aurelia—"

"It's not a big deal!" she snapped. She stood up, looking around at the books on the floor. "We did a lot of work anyway. I'll talk to you tomorrow, okay?"

Chloe bit her lip. She wanted so badly to say something, anything. But there was nothing to say. Instead, she simply stood and offered what she hoped was a pleasant goodbye before turning to leave.

Once outside, she ducked between the same two houses she had after her first visit. Somehow she found the energy to pull her from Aurelia's house to her own.

She staggered through the doorway, lurching for the book that described the different supernatural families. She dragged it to her bed, and, propped against the pillows, scanned a page of psychics she'd paid no mind to before.

Smiling triumphantly, she laid the open book on the floor and sank back into the plush embrace of the mattress.

Within moments, she was asleep.

THIRTEEN

The next morning, she felt significantly better than she had the day before. Partly due to the fact she'd fallen asleep before the sun had finished going down, but mostly due to renewed inspiration. She couldn't pinpoint the range of Aurelia's powers yet, but she knew where they came from.

"Aleksi Olivette," was written in a loose scrawl, staring up at her from the page she'd left open the night before, and followed by a vague note: "Dreams?"

He'd been the last in a long line of thought manipulators. It was a long shot—there was clearly no confirmation on Aleksi Olivette, and his entry came several generations before Aurelia—but it was as close as anything listed in the book. And if the abilities had had several generations to mutate, adapting to include more than just dreams . . . well, that could describe Aurelia perfectly.

She had no idea how thought manipulation might help resurrect a set of ancient demons, but that was no matter. She'd solved the mystery. Alex and Rus could—and would—in their quest to hoard all dangerous, glamorous, or interesting tasks, take it from there.

She slipped her shoes on, a feeling of triumph hovering in her chest and clouding her sense of time. She clicked the front door shut a full ten minutes before she would usually consider leaving and ended up arriving at school the same time as Aurelia.

She waved merrily, pausing in front of the entrance as the girl approached from the opposite direction. There'd been a lingering awkwardness the last time Aurelia's powers emerged; her goal this morning was to ensure that didn't happen again.

"Hey!" she said brightly.

Aurelia gave a weak, early-morning smile. "Hey. Did you get some sleep?"

"Oh, yeah. More than I needed, maybe," Chloe answered, forcing out a giggle. "I was thinking we could try the project again tonight?"

"Uh. Sure, yeah," Aurelia said, looking a little surprised.

"Your place, again? I was thinking—"

"Chloe?" a voice called from behind her.

She recognized that rough, gravelly tenor; it was the last voice she expected to hear at a human high school. She turned around, confirming her suspicions.

Lounging against a scrubby tree stood her brother Mikhail.

He looked the same as the last time she'd seen him—quite a bit like her. They shared the same straight, narrow features, though his jaw was squared off in a way that favored their father. His hair was the same dark, straight sort as hers, but kept much shorter, falling in shaggy fashion to just below his ears. The only striking difference, aside from gender, was the alert hazel in his eyes instead of her icy blue.

He'd had the decency to wear a soft, brown button-up with sleeves long enough to cover the majority of his tattoos. But she could still see dark bands of pattern and jagged scars creeping out from beneath the cuffs.

For a moment, she simply gawked at him before dashing

forward and flinging her arms around his neck. "Mikhail! What are you doing here?"

Aurelia followed, cocking her head to the side. "This is your brother?"

Mikhail gave Chloe a faint squeeze before gently pushing her away. He gave her a small, half smile. "I came to check on you, of course." To Aurelia, he offered a nod. "Hey. Mikhail."

"Aurelia," she replied, the corners of her lips tugging upward.

Chloe frowned. "Check on me?"

"Our cousins mentioned you might need it," he said lightly.

She scowled. "They mentioned I *might* need it, so you came all the way back from—"

"Hey, hey," he said gently, shooting Aurelia an apologetic sort of look. He grabbed Chloe's upper arm, pulling her a few steps away from the other girl. "Look, I didn't just come back for this, okay?"

She studied him, her eyes narrowed. "You're going to help them channel."

He shrugged.

"God, they're getting so desperate . . ."

"From what I've heard, you're not doing much to help that," Mikhail said shortly. "Still running around with vampires, getting yourself into all sorts of trouble. Alex and Rus could really use some help, you know."

She crossed her arms indignantly. "That's not all I've been doing!" At his serious expression, she sighed. "It's not like they tell me much. I've been doing what they asked, okay? I'm here, figuring that girl out."

"She's part of it?" he asked, shooting a quick glance at Aurelia. "That's too bad.

Chloe bit her lip. "The thing is . . . I don't think she is. I mean, the Ways say so, but . . ."

"But what?" Mikhail said dryly. "If the Ways have directed you to her, it's obviously for a reason—"

"This isn't something I want to discuss here," she cut in sharply, looking over his shoulder to the waiting Aurelia. The girl was looking at them curiously, rocking up and down on the balls of her feet.

Mikhail released a heavy sigh. He grabbed her arm again and pulled her back toward the human girl, a wide smile on his face.

"Aurelia, it was so nice to meet you. I'm sorry to take your friend away, but I've really missed my sister. I think she might just have to miss a few classes so I can take her out to breakfast." He winked as he slung a thick arm over Chloe's shoulders.

She instantly plastered the same smile on her face, wondering what it said about her, that all of her family and most of the people she encountered were such smooth, casual liars. Maybe it just came with the whole supernatural schtick.

Aurelia shifted her backpack, giving an uncertain smile. "Oh . . . uh . . . okay. I guess I can, uh, get the work for you, Chloe."

She was about to tell her not to bother, but Mikhail spoke first. "That would be great, Aurelia."

The warning bell sounded from the depths of the building. Aurelia looked back at the entrance and then to Chloe. "Well, uh, all right. I guess I'll see you later."

"Yeah, later," Chloe agreed, giving a small wave.

Aurelia disappeared into the building.

"Let's find somewhere you *will* be comfortable." Mikhail muttered, guiding her away from the school.

※

It felt strange to Chloe, sitting in the small café she'd only ever frequented with Aurelia, poking at a slightly soggy breakfast sandwich.

Even though Mikhail was here, sitting across from her, gnawing at a breakfast wrap of his own, he still felt so far away. After she'd stopped hunting, she'd had the fleeting thought that perhaps he was someone she could talk to, could explain her thinking to. But now that he was in front of her, she felt nothing but a lump in her throat and a vague anxiety about how he would react.

As if following her line of thought, he swallowed and sighed. "Enough, Chloe. You have to start talking about something that matters."

The entire walk over, she'd babbled about the inconsequential happenings in her life to try and quell her nerves—dreaming about their parents, missing him, the town of Molten. But she'd skipped right over the important factors: Ducante. Josef. Aurelia.

She took a deep breath. Aurelia. Start with Aurelia. "I don't think she's part of it, Mikhail."

"You said that," he answered smoothly, taking a long sip of coffee. "But I've heard no reason why."

"How could she be?" Chloe said seriously, pushing the sandwich away.

Mikhail sighed again, pinching the bridge of his nose between two fingers. It was a habit he'd had since the disappearance of their parents. "We don't even know what she can do. How can we just discount her?"

"She . . ." Chloe paused, eyes darting around the restaurant. It was empty save for a bored-looking, definitely-human cashier fiddling with their phone. "Does something with thoughts."

"There's a lot you can do with thoughts."

"Well, that's just it, isn't it?" Chloe hissed. "She can't really *do* anything. She can hear them—other people's, I mean—sometimes, but she can't control it and she doesn't understand it. How is she part of bringing *them* back?"

Mikhail sighed, running a hand through his shaggy hair. "I don't know, Chloe, but we don't have much else to go on."

"Nothing at all?"

He shook his head. "Whoever is behind this has taken every precaution. They're well hidden, and we're running out of resources."

Chloe bit her lip. This would be the perfect time to mention Josef. "What if we tried to talk to other . . . you know . . . people?" She glanced at the human behind the counter.

"No one is talking," he said quietly. "Believe me, I've visited almost all my sources."

Her mind flashed to the night at Ducante's, to Cain. She wondered if they'd spoken recently, if Mikhail knew about their meeting.

"We could really use your help channeling, you know," he added.

"But I thought you said Aurelia was all we—"

He held up a hand, cutting her off. "Yes, the girl is all we have *for now*. But until she does something more than pick up a few errant thoughts, you can spare some energy to help us find something bigger."

"I have to help by *channeling*?"

"Do you have any better ideas?"

She squirmed in her seat. "I'm getting close to figuring out the extent of her powers. I can't just leave now.

Mikhail steepled his hands on the table, his hazel eyes fixed on her in a pensive reverie. After a beat, he spoke. "You can miss today—the girl isn't going to change in a day."

The lump in Chloe's throat tightened. She'd hoped to get out of channeling altogether. The idea of touching the Ways, the things she'd avoided despite specific instruction, made the salty café fare in her stomach curdle.

"All right," she said with a slow nod. "All right."

ᢧ

She'd forgotten how much channeling hurt—especially with four Naimei gathered around the Ways. The thrum of power that coursed through them unsettled and comforted her at the same time, making her head spin.

No one had seemed especially interested in what she had to offer about Aurelia; to them, it was just another disappointing dead end. Alex had regarded her with the same arm's-length attitude he addressed everyone with. Mikhail gave her a nod and a quick pat on the shoulder. And Rus had given her a long, lingering stare—the first since his encounter with Sam—but hadn't said anything. Luckily, they'd begun channeling before that stare could break her into admitting all the secrets she'd been keeping.

The Ways hummed and whirred as magic and focus were poured into them, but the channeling itself was no help. The silver instruments seemed unable to make up their minds. They spun helter-skelter, tilting this way and that, never pausing long enough to gain a clear read, changing too often for anything to be reliable. Chloe held her breath, her face turning purple as she tried to impose her powers on the silver tools. She could have sworn the node for proximity pointed north-west longer than the other directions. Then she exhaled, and it was lost.

When Alex finally signaled for them to withdraw their powers, they'd gained nothing but aching muscles. Chloe was shaking so badly she collapsed into one of Rus and Alex's old couches, gnawing on a hunk of bread and sipping the pungent tea they offered her.

"Take a day to rest," Alex advised, surveying Chloe's pallid form, "and we'll resume day after tomorrow."

Rus gave a grim nod. Mikhail grunted, tearing off a piece of bread for himself.

Chloe wondered, not for the first time, what good it would do if the Ways continued to fail. How much time did they actually have left?

❧

Chloe spent the first few hours of the next day trying to formulate a plan. Her head was still spinning from channeling, and Alex had made it clear as they'd left that they would channel for as long as it took; meaning her contact with Aurelia was on the verge of ending. She didn't want to be pulled away from the only semblance of action she was allowed to see just so she could stare at hunks of metal. But despite what she'd told Mikhail, she wasn't at all sure how close she was to discovering Aurelia's secrets. She had a better hint now, yes, but the girl's powers had proved almost impossible to draw out, and she still doubted their relevance.

The two times Aurelia had slipped up had been when she was off guard. Either because she was relaxed, or too busy thinking about something else. Chloe's best option, then, was to distract her in the hope she'd do something that qualified as supernatural. But how?

Her gaze landed on Aurelia's open notebook.

"What are you drawing?" she asked carefully.

The girl shrugged, tilting the notebook up to squint at the lines. "I don't know. I had a dream about it last night. Maybe it's a city, or something? I'm not really sure."

Chloe gaped at her, at the squiggles she'd created. As crude as the drawing was, there was absolutely no doubt it was the

Ways. Not the perfectly balanced version from when her parents had Vanished, but exactly as they'd sat on her kitchen table the night Alex had assembled them.

"You *dreamed* about that?" Chloe asked softly. Her mouth had gone dry.

Aurelia shrugged again. "There might have been some people, too . . . sitting in a circle, or something. I couldn't really tell."

"Where's the closest phone?" she interrupted.

"I . . . I think there's a payphone outside the cafeteria? No one uses it, though," Aurelia said, confused. "Chloe, what's—"

"I'll be right back!" she said, dashing out of Study Hall.

She made a mental note to thank Aurelia for directing her to the right place: a navy blue payphone sat exactly where she'd said it would. She paused, trying to remember Alex's number before pushing the correct buttons.

The phone rang once, twice, with only the vaguest crackle of technological protest. She hoped Mikhail was still there, that he'd be the one to pick up. Three, four . . .

"Hello?"

"Mikhail?" Chloe said desperately. "Look, something changed."

"Chloe, what . . . ?"

"Not now! I just, I need you to meet me somewhere." She twisted the cord around her finger. Aurelia drawing the Ways . . . it was exactly what she'd needed. The final puzzle piece.

There was a pause on the line. "Chloe, what happened?"

"I'll show you! Meet me somewhere . . . somewhere . . . high school friendly," she added.

"Did you have a place in mind?"

Chloe racked her brain, trying to think of somewhere two supernaturals and whatever Aurelia was could meet in semi-privacy. Somewhere familiar, that she could get to quickly . . .

157

"Ducante's. Ducante's bar; it's downtown, by all those fancy restaurants."

"Ducante's? That's hardly high school friendly. How do you even know about that place?"

"Just meet me there, okay?"

Another pause. "Fine. Twenty minutes."

The conversation clicked off.

Chloe placed the receiver in the cradle and returned to Study Hall. Aurelia was still puzzling over her drawing, as if searching for something offensive and coming up wanting.

"Chloe, hey, look, I don't know what's up but—"

"What do you say we cut some classes today?" Chloe said quickly.

A look of shock crossed Aurelia's face. "I—"

"It'll be fun!" Chloe trilled, pulling Aurelia to her feet. "Think of it as an extended lunch. Bring that notebook you were drawing in."

"I guess—" Aurelia started again.

Chloe put on her best smile. "Great," she said, guiding the girl from the room before she had time to realize it was nowhere near lunch.

Luckily, Study Hall was, for the most part, entirely unsupervised. They left unnoticed, and were out of the building before Aurelia tugged at Chloe's arm, clutching a stitch in her side.

"God, slow down a little. Where are we even going?"

Chloe bit her lip. "Uh, that place. You know, the one Josef met me at."

"Ducante's?" Aurelia asked incredulously. "We're going to have an extended lunch at a *bar*? Are you crazy?"

"No, look, it'll be fun. My brother wants to meet up with us—"

"Your brother?" It was Aurelia's turn to interrupt. "Why does he want to meet us?"

"Uh," Chloe said, scrambling for a response. "Uh. To hang out. With me. And, uh, with you."

To her surprise, a bit of red flowed into Aurelia's cheeks.

"Oh," the girl said softly.

Chloe half pulled, half dragged Aurelia downtown. By the time they reached Ducante's, the girl was panting in earnest, but Chloe didn't pause; she simply tugged open the door.

Just like her Sunday afternoon visit, the bar was utterly deserted. But then, it was a Monday before noon. Ducante was seated at the bar itself, paging through the stack of paperwork Chloe'd seen the other day. He had a pen tucked neatly behind one ear, and was holding a glass of the same burgundy liquid she'd seen him drinking her first trip.

"Ah," he glanced up with a slightly surprised expression. "Well, if it isn't Chloe Naimei. And a friend," he said curiously, raising an eyebrow at Aurelia's presence.

"Is he going to check our I.D.'s?" Aurelia hissed, probably suspecting "Naimei" to be a name read on a fake.

She sighed. "Why don't you go get a table? I'll get us drinks and . . . uh . . . food." She thought she'd seen a human eating some sort of pub fare on one of her previous visits but now that she thought about it, she couldn't actually remember if they served food or not.

Aurelia shuffled off, selecting a table smack in the middle of all the empty ones, as if they would somehow shield her underage status from the owner. Chloe shook her head, and headed for the bar. Ducante had resumed his usual place behind it, shuffling the papers he'd been looking at. They appeared to be nothing more than particularly mundane expense reports.

"So, my dear," Ducante began, "What brings you here today? Some new form of revenge? Filling my bar with underage girls to get my liquor license revoked?"

"I suppose that's one way to look at it," Chloe said, sliding onto a stool while carefully avoiding the edge of the bar. "But no, that's not why I'm here. Remember when you said not to come back until I needed a supernatural meeting place?"

Ducante gave a slow nod.

"Well . . ." she trailed off with a shrug.

He arched one eyebrow, running a hand through his hair. "That's all fine and good," he lowered his voice conspiratorially, "But I hate to tell you that you came in with a human."

Chloe raised an eyebrow, mimicking his expression, leaning in as close as she dared. "Did I?" she asked in a low, provocative voice.

Ducante gave a sharp bark of laughter. "Suit yourself, Chloe. But if this has anything to do with certain recent events we've disagreed on, I will have to reiterate that you're wasting your time—especially on a human." He chuckled, pulling two glasses from behind the bar. "What can I get you?"

"Something normal," Chloe replied blandly.

Ducante squinted at Aurelia and shook his head with a sigh. Grabbing the soda gun, he filled the glasses with some sort of cola before adding a thimbleful of rum to each.

"Will that do?" When Chloe wrinkled her nose at the alcohol, he rolled his eyes, adding, "It's solely for tongue-loosening purposes, of course."

"I'd hope so," she said, gathering up the glasses. "Oh. Hey. Do you serve food?"

He crossed his arms over his chest, fixing her with a serious expression. "What sort of business do you think I'm running? Of course we serve food," he said, tossing a leather-bound menu onto the bar in front of her. "But the cook isn't in until the afternoon." A smirk fell over his lips. "I would offer to prepare something myself, but I imagine our tastes differ quite drastically."

The way he said it made the hair on the back of her neck

stand on end. She was grappling with a response when Ducante chuckled again.

"I suppose I could order a pizza," he said with a wink.

She gave an appreciative smile and retreated to the table Aurelia had chosen. As she passed the drinks over, the girl looked at her with wide, surprised eyes, abandoning the drawing she'd resumed doodling in.

"Rum and coke," Chloe said.

"He served you *alcohol?*" Aurelia squeaked. "Do you *know* him?"

She shrugged, nudging the drink closer. "Friend of a friend. Or something. Oh, and all they have is pizza. I hope you don't mind."

Aurelia shook her head as she took a furtive sip. "God. I can't believe I'm skipping class to drink in a bar . . . and, and it's not even eleven-thirty yet."

The door banged open. Chloe jerked her gaze up: it should have been either her brother or the pizza delivery guy, but she was surprised to see a very disoriented Sam, looking as pale as the day he'd wound up on her doorstep. Mikhail, face contorted in disdain, followed closely behind him.

Ducante's face seemed to drain of life. There was a distinct shattering noise as the glass he'd been polishing dropped to the ground.

"Chl-Chloe," Sam said through chattering teeth. He shook his head, as if trying to shake something away, his whole body shuddering visibly.

Mikhail pushed the vampire forward, turning his dissatisfied expression on her. "I found *this* on my way to meet you. You two seem to know each other?"

Sam stumbled and collapsed, grasping at his hair. Aurelia jumped out of her chair, taking a few steps back. "What . . . Sam . . . what is he . . . what the . . . ?"

"How the *hell* is he still alive?" Ducante demanded.

161

Chloe tore her gaze away from Sam and looked up at him. He'd abandoned his post behind the bar to stand nearby, staring down at the writhing boy with what appeared to be great trepidation. "What are you talking about, 'still alive'? Did you have something to do with his poisoning?"

"Of course I did, you idiot girl," he growled. "I was repairing a situation you Naimei seem unequipped to deal with properly."

Whatever Mikhail might have known about Ducante's bar, he clearly knew very little of the proprietor; at the word "Naimei", a knife appeared in his hand and he dropped into a fighting stance.

Ducante bared his teeth, displaying their true razor-edged appearance. The brown of his eyes slid back to reveal their natural, blood red.

Mikhail's eyes widened. He sucked in a sharp breath, but whatever he'd been about to say was cut off by a small shriek from Aurelia.

"Damn it, Chloe, why did you bring her here?" Mikhail snapped.

In answer, Chloe picked up the notebook and flung it toward her brother. It sailed easily over Sam, who was rocking back and forth on the floor, his hands still tangled in his dark tresses.

Mikhail caught the flapping paper easily with his free hand. He looked down at the drawing, and his brow furrowed. Ignoring Ducante, he looked up at Aurelia.

"You drew this?" he said in a level voice. Though devoid of accusation or anger, in his gravelly tone, it was still quite intimidating.

Aurelia's gray eyes flickered from Mikhail, to the notebook, to the knife. Meeting his gaze, she nodded slowly. "I . . . I dreamt about it. I don't know what it is, I swear!"

"I told you she could do something with thoughts," Chloe said. "I fell asleep around her and she could see what I was dreaming. But there's no way she could know how the Ways looked a week ago—"

"Thought-weaver," Mikhail said softly, still studying the drawing. "I didn't think they actually existed, but . . . if she pulled this out . . ."

"What does that mean?" Chloe asked.

Her brother shook his head slowly. "A lot of things. She would be able to tap into people's minds, a true two-way connection, and pull out thoughts, memories. Organize them as needed. But I don't—"

A gargled shout cut through the room, interrupting Mikhail and pulling all eyes toward Sam. The vampire had gone still. He stared straight ahead, his dark eyes wide. Words fell quickly from his lips, but they were from no language Chloe recognized.

Ducante seemed positively distraught. His eyes were flickering between red and brown, like he was unable to control it. "Shut him up! Damn it, shut him up!"

"You understand him? What's he saying?" Chloe asked, moving forward to kneel beside Sam. She reached out, placing a hand on his back, but it had as much effect as a gnat landing on a lion. Though she couldn't understand what he was mumbling, she could hear a pattern in the sounds, as if he was repeating some sort of mantra.

"That language . . ." Ducante spat in a choked voice, "Has not been uttered for a millennia. He's channeling forces of purest evil. Finish what I started and kill him. Now!"

Mikhail stepped forward, but Chloe held up a panicked hand. "No! No, wait. We can use this to our advantage. Ducante, what is he channeling?"

Ducante, muttering darkly under his breath, turned and angrily kicked a bar stool. It flew into a wall, leaving a sizeable dent. Aurelia let out a whimper and sank into a nearby chair.

"He can't be," Mikhail said. Chloe looked up at him, but

his gaze was focused on Ducante. "That line died out long ago. There's no way he could possibly be . . ."

Ducante spat on the floor, wiping his mouth with the back of his hand before he replied. "He is. The last of the line of vampires started by Pan and Damonos. His youth kept him hidden until very recently."

Chloe felt her eyes widen as she looked between the two. "What? What does that mean? Are they . . . are they possessing him?"

The bar owner snorted. "If only it were that easy. Coming out of wherever Pan and Damonos have been lurking all these years requires much more than possession; they're using him to convey a message. Instructions. For whoever's been trying to resurrect them. They'll use this vampire, their last blood connection, to complete the ritual and find suitable forms for them to manifest in. He will be their sacrifice."

A shiver quaked down Chloe's spine.

"So he'll die anyway," Mikhail said.

"No!" Chloe shouted, standing. "No. We can do something about this! We don't know what killing him will do. What if we inadvertently complete the sacrifice?"

Her brother shifted his weight from foot to foot, suddenly looking uncomfortable.

"We have to try and fix this," she insisted.

"This is beyond your power to fix, Naimei," Ducante said firmly. "They will be tightening their grip on him, now. They'll erase everything he is to ensure he completes the task at hand. His mind will only know his duty as sacrifice."

Chloe looked to her brother for confirmation. Mikhail's eyes darted to where Aurelia sat slumped in a chair, her gaze focused on the still-chanting Sam. Of course—*thought*-weaver.

Chloe bit down on her lip. "Aurelia?" she said gently.

The girl jerked as if she'd been slapped. Her eyes flitted around the room; she looked as much like a deer in headlights as anyone Chloe had ever seen. "What's happening?" Aurelia asked.

"I know there's a lot to take in right now. We don't have time to explain, but we're going to need your help to—"

"Things have always happened to you that you can't explain," Mikhail said sharply, cutting her off. "Haven't they?"

Aurelia fixed him with a hard, steady stare. Chloe cringed; going at things so directly was almost never the answer. She was prepared for Aurelia to deny his accusation, to run screaming from the bar, but instead, to her amazement, the girl gave a slow, minute nod.

"What you can do is unique," Mikhail continued. "The human mind . . . it's like a book to you. Except you can make edits, sort through, rearrange. You can help us fix this." He nodded toward Sam. "Will you?"

The girl stared at him for a moment. Her gaze moved to Chloe, Ducante, Sam, and then back to Mikhail. She bit her lip, shifting in her chair. "I . . . I don't know what to do. I don't think I can."

"You can," he said firmly. "I can help you." He took a few steps forward, gesturing for her to do the same.

Slowly, Aurelia obeyed. They knelt on either side of the chanting vampire. Ducante scowled, lashing out at another stool, catching it with his arm and flinging it into a wall. "You'll trust an untrained, untried human with the fate of the world? This is absolute *madness*."

"That's something, coming from you," Chloe said snidely.

His lip curled. His teeth were still in their horrible, razor-sharp form. "Just because I appreciate chaos does not mean I lust for all levels of it, Naimei."

"Shut up, both of you," Mikhail snapped before trying to level his expression into something resembling calm. "All right, Aurelia. You were listening while we were talking?"

"S-sort of," she stuttered.

"Okay. There are things in Sam's mind that shouldn't be. That's what's making him like this. We need you to pull them out—and you *can* do that—so he can go back to normal. Once he does, we'll start explaining things. Sound good?"

Aurelia took a deep, rattling breath, and swallowed. "What do I do?"

Mikhail explained how to place her hands on Sam's temples for maximum connection, explained what it would feel like, what she would look for. Carefully, hands shaking, she did as she was told.

At first, nothing happened. Chloe became aware that she was tapping her foot impatiently and made a conscious effort to hold it still. Across the room, Ducante was drumming his fingers on the gleaming surface of the bar.

Aurelia looked confused, but just as she opened her mouth to speak, her expression changed. It relaxed. Her mouth closed, her eyes shut.

Mikhail began whispering gentle encouragements, suggestions, though if Aurelia was able to hear him, she gave no indication. Nor did Sam.

The chanting became more frantic. Chloe hoped that was a good sign.

Aurelia stayed like that—eyes shut, stationary, hands resting on Sam's temples—for what seemed like an eternity. Gradually, his chanting slowed. Then stopped altogether. Chloe felt her heart flutter. *She did it,* she thought.

Aurelia's eyes snapped open. They were wide, glazed, fixed on everything and nothing all at once. Chloe felt her stomach sink.

"When night becomes even with day, we pass through bodies that hold worlds to find true forms. Through energy and bloom, we return to this world. Bound, by the sacrifice of our blood, to the one who calls us. When night becomes even with day . . ."

The voice she was speaking in was no voice Chloe had ever heard Aurelia use. It sounded strangely disembodied; unearthly, even.

"What's happening?" Chloe asked desperately.

Aurelia was shaking.

"I think . . . I think in trying to get rid of everything, she had to take some of it into herself," Mikhail said, his eyes widening as Aurelia started the third repetition of the mantra.

"Is that what Sam's been saying the whole time?" Chloe whispered, looking at Ducante.

Ducante's lips had pressed into a thin line. He looked grim.

". . . we return to this world for the one who calls us." Aurelia's shaking had grown so severe Chloe was sure she'd break something if it continued. Just as she took the first step forward to intervene, however, Aurelia stopped, jerking her hands away from Sam. The motion seemed to take an amazing feat of strength.

Sam collapsed onto the ground, unconscious, and Aurelia scrambled to put distance between herself and the vampire.

"Aurelia?" Chloe asked tentatively.

The girl looked around. Her eyes seemed wild, her hair disheveled from all the shaking. "Did you hear everything? You had to hear everything."

"We did," Chloe said slowly.

"And . . . and . . . he's really, he's a . . ." she stuttered, her eyes flickering to Sam.

"Yes," Chloe said quickly. "He's a vampire."

"And . . . and . . ." her eyes darted around the bar, taking in the people around her.

"Yes," Mikhail said, without waiting for Aurelia to ask the question. "It's all real."

The girl's lip quivered. Chloe opened her mouth to say something, anything, that might help her process the situation, but Aurelia spoke first. "After . . . after all these years. . . I always knew something . . . was different . . . *I* was different . . . it all makes sense now."

She burst into a frantic fit of tears.

FOURTEEN

It took a full ten minutes to calm Aurelia down. At one point, Ducante suggested a glass of ice water to the face—or head—might silence her screaming. Chloe summoned her most malevolent look in response. He muttered something about finding the food he'd ordered for them and slunk out of the bar, reappearing only after Aurelia's fit had been reduced to the occasional sniffle.

Chloe handed her another napkin. She accepted it with a mumbled, "Thank you," wiping at her tear-stained cheeks.

Ducante tossed a pizza box onto the bar and approached, a plastic cup of steaming liquid in his hand. He held it out to Aurelia. She took it cautiously, holding it like a lifeline.

Though calm, she still seemed to be in a minor state of shock. She asked a few questions, accepting the answers with a small nod. Apparently, the still-unconscious Sam had provided a lot of information when she tapped into his mind.

She already seemed to know quite a bit about vampires, and had some idea of what Chloe and Mikhail were. "So . . . you guys . . . you can do magic?" she asked tentatively.

"Sort of," Mikhail replied. Ducante laughed sharply. Her cheeks went red and she let the subject drop.

Ducante seemed to be the only one that made her nervous.

She'd no doubt concluded exactly what he was, though she didn't ask about demons and no one mentioned them.

For the most part, they avoided questioning her directly. There was no mention of Pan and Damonos or the disembodied voice that had spilled from her mouth. They let her process everything, answering questions and explaining until, eventually, Aurelia seemed to fade. Chloe decided that food would probably help and went to divvy up the pizza. Once the girl was stable, they could get to the important stuff.

When she opened the pizza box, Ducante pulled a face at the cooked-food smell. He vanished into a back room and returned with an extremely raw-looking steak and a glass filled with the burgundy liquid he was so fond of drinking. Chloe scowled at him.

"Get over yourself," she said, sliding the pizza slices onto several cocktail napkins.

"Hey now, Sweetheart, I'll have you remember this is *my* bar you're making an absolute mockery of," he replied, meticulously cutting the steak into small pieces. It oozed blood onto the white plate.

"I thought you would appreciate us saving the day," she quipped, picking up the pizza-laden napkins.

He rolled his eyes. "You haven't saved anything yet. In fact, you did the opposite by not letting that vampire die. All you're doing is grasping at straws while you try to make amends." Ducante took a long draught of burgundy liquid.

Chloe frowned. "Whatever. What is that you're always drinking?" she asked, trying to change the subject.

Ducante swallowed and raised an eyebrow. "Do you really want the answer to that?" he said darkly.

She decided she didn't and elected, instead, to take the pizza to Mikhail and Aurelia, who'd been discussing yet another of her many questions.

Mikhail ignored the food, but Aurelia accepted a piece to nibble on experimentally. After a few bites, she began to eat in earnest. Chloe followed her example and took a few polite bites of her own slice, keeping quiet as the girl recovered.

Her brother, however, was not so patient.

"Aurelia," he began as she took her last few bites of pizza, "We need to talk about what happened while you were in Sam's mind. What happened and . . . what you said." Chloe gave Mikhail one of the looks she'd been reserving for Ducante.

Aurelia wadded up her greasy cocktail napkin. Then, slowly, she nodded.

"Is Sam going to be okay?" Chloe blurted out. The pale, dark-haired boy was still unconscious where he'd fallen. He'd been in a similar state after she'd healed him, but it hadn't lasted for so long.

"Oh. Yes!" Aurelia said quickly, brightening at a topic she clearly hadn't been expecting. "At least, I think so. This was my first time—"

"That's all fine and good," Mikhail interrupted, frowning at Chloe, "but what we really need to talk about is what you said."

"I . . . I'm glad you heard it," Aurelia muttered, picking at a chip in the wood table. "It . . . it seemed important."

Chloe leaned forward. "It is important. Do you have any idea what it meant? Was there anything else in Sam's head, any other clues?"

Aurelia said nothing. She stared off into the distance, her gaze focused somewhere between where she sat and the door.

"It's fine," Mikhail offered after a derisive snort from Ducante. "We can work with what we have to figure out when, where and who—"

"How?" Ducante snapped from behind the bar. "You idiots didn't even know *that* was involved," he gestured to Sam, then Aurelia, "and didn't realize what *she* could do until just now. I'll bet you still have no idea why she fits into all this, do you?"

Chloe wanted so badly for Mikhail to have a witty retort, because she had none. Ducante was right. She was glad to have discovered Aurelia's capabilities—and that she was no longer stuck constantly lying to the girl—but how she fit into a mysterious plot to raise two ancient demons, she still had no idea. Aurelia wouldn't have even known it was happening if not for Sam's surprise presence in the bar.

"I thought so," Ducante said in a superior tone.

"Why don't you enlighten us, then, if you're so smart?" Chloe countered.

He crossed his arms, leaning against the back shelf of the bar. "The answers are so obvious that I'll tell you solely out of pity." He flicked a piece of lint from his shirt sleeve. "Think about it. Wherever these demons are, they're clearly unable to come into our world on their own, or they'd be here already. They must need a form—bodies.

"Given the limited number of supernaturals, odds are they'll wind up in humans. And that will most likely render their powers severely diminished, if not entirely useless, since the human mind would be utterly unable to comprehend them."

"So, what? They want Aurelia's powers? Or . . . her body?" Chloe asked. Aurelia shuddered in her chair.

Ducante let out another snort. "Of course not. What are her powers compared to those of demons as old as the world? No, I doubt they want anything more than to use her. If she can get in their minds, she could reorganize them and give back their powers regardless of form."

"Thought-weavers are rare, but I've never known any to possess that kind of power," Mikhail said skeptically.

"Of course you haven't," Ducante said, rolling his eyes; they'd finally resumed their standard, chocolate-brown hue. "They'd never really have a reason to try, now, would they? But she successfully transferred and removed a channeling energy from what might have been worlds away just by pulling it out of his blood. I don't doubt what she's capable of."

Slowly, all eyes turned to Aurelia. She shifted in her chair, dropping her gaze toward the gleaming floor. She mumbled something about it not being true, about being sorry for what was happening, but at the volume she was speaking, it was nearly indiscernible.

Ducante laughed. "This is what you have to work with—an unconscious vampire and a human girl who only learned about our world today. And you expect to find a time, location, and person responsible *before* Pan and Damonos are walking among us?" he shook his head, letting out another laugh. He plucked a bottle off one of the shelves and took a long swig. "We're all doomed."

"I'd bet anything you know who's responsible," Mikhail growled. "If you'd cooperate, we'd at least have that."

Ducante's eyes narrowed in a way that made Chloe's stomach drop to her toes. She'd seen that look before, and what came next wasn't pretty. When he spoke, his voice was a barely controlled whisper. "Do you not think I would tell you if I knew *anything* that could actually be used?"

No one spoke. Chloe felt uneasy; she'd never known how she felt about Gregory Ducante, but had always viewed him as non-threatening, somehow. This morning's events seemed to unhinge him, though. Anything might bring about the reaction she'd witnessed during their last encounter, and with her brother, an unconscious Sam, and Aurelia nearby, that was not a scenario she wanted to see.

"I . . . I know when. And where," Aurelia said quietly. Chloe, along with everyone else, gaped at the girl in disbelief. "The Spring Fling Dance. Saturday."

"Aurelia," Chloe said gently, "why would two demons decide to re-enter our world at a high school dance? That doesn't mean anything to them. I'm sure you were just confusing Sam's thoughts with your own."

"No!" she said firmly. "No. I saw it. In . . . in his mind. It was just a quick image, but I knew it looked familiar. The botanical gardens—that's where it's going to happen. It was all dark, like it was night."

"'When night becomes even with day,'" Mikhail repeated slowly. "The spring equinox is this Saturday. Night and day would be perfectly even."

"It still doesn't make sense," Chloe argued, trying to keep her voice level. "Why would it happen at a botanical garden north of Molton? Don't you think the location is a little random? The person trying to bring them back is pretty powerful, right? Wouldn't we have noticed something?"

"Not if someone is hiding their presence," Mikhail said quietly. "It's difficult, but I've known witches who can make a centuries-old vampire feel like nothing more than a kitten."

"So is it a vampire?" Chloe asked. "Or . . . or a witch? Or . . . ?" She glanced toward Ducante.

He sighed in response. "Contrary to popular belief, there is no underground demon network where we share evil plans, Sweetheart." When she continued to stare at him, he added, "Few of us lust for the chaos that used to exist in this world, and I know of no others in the immediate area of Molton, if that's what you're asking."

Mikhail sighed, running a hand through his shaggy hair. The tattoos on his arms rippled with the motion. "If they're strong enough to pull Pan and Damonos from wherever they are . . . I doubt we'd be able to find them easily anyway. Even channeling, the Ways are useless; it's the first time I've ever seen them con-fused. Which brings us back to why Molton."

"There was . . . that one phrase," Chloe said, drumming her fingers on the table. "'We pass through bodies that hold worlds . . .'"

"What does that mean?" Aurelia asked, her brows furrowed in concentration.

"Well, it could mean they literally need to travel through bodies to enter the world," Mikhail explained with a nod toward Ducante, "But 'bodies that hold worlds' could also be a lot of other things; big things that run deep into other planes of exist-ence—rivers, for example, or the tallest mountains. They're . . . passages, of sorts."

"There's nothing like that in Molton," Chloe complained. "It's all but flat. The Mississippi is the biggest body in North America, and we're nowhere near it."

Ducante let out a, "Hmph," and walked quickly through a doorway to the side of the bar. There was the faint sound of banging—drawers slamming, papers rustling—before he re-emerged carrying several rolls of paper. He marched to their table, knocking the remaining bits of pizza to the ground in order to lay the papers out.

They appeared to be maps of some sort, though they documented much more than streets and buildings. There were deeper schematics—power lines, utilities—all marked in a color-coded key.

"What is this?" Chloe asked, pausing over a spot she was sure was Molton Area High School.

Ducante shrugged, tracing one finger on the map. "Schematics. Blue prints. Molton," he added, with a gesture toward the page.

"Why do you have them?" Mikhail asked suspiciously. Chloe noticed he'd never put his knife away, and at Ducante's approach, his grip on it tightened.

"Potential business ventures," Ducante said coolly, not bothering to look up from the map. "I was considering developing land, and a lot of it comes with . . . ah. Here," he said, pointing to a long, thick band of blue that ran north from just beyond the high school, through the edges of the city, and off the map entirely.

Chloe frowned, but it was Aurelia who spoke first. "Is that supposed to be a river? There's nothing like that in Molton."

"Ah," Ducante said serenely, "but there is *underneath* Molton. Quite deep, if memory serves me correctly. It's fairly large—runs into an underground reservoir on the far, north-side of town. The reservoir is closer to the surface than any other point in the system. A lot of the land up there is fed by well water—including the botanical gardens, I'd imagine."

"So the whole area . . ." Mikhail said, drifting off.

Ducante nodded. "Is fed by a large, deep water system. A 'body', if you will."

Aurelia's gray eyes were wide with shock. She'd been right.

Chloe shook her head in protest. "That still doesn't make sense. These are powerful demons we're talking about. Why wouldn't they come back at a bigger source? Somewhere more magically revered?"

The demon sighed, tapping his temple impatiently. "Think, Naimei, *think*. They left this world hundreds of thousands of years ago. That body would have been much bigger, much closer to the surface—in fact, wherever they've been sent, it might *still* be on the surface."

She pressed her lips into a thin line. "'Through energy and bloom . . .'"

Mikhail shook his head slowly, pinching the bridge of his nose. "Christ. The botanical garden does make sense."

Aurelia looked around at the three faces huddled over the table. "So . . . so what does this mean?"

Chloe shut her eyes, massaging her temples gently. "It means . . . we're *all* going to the Spring Fling Dance," she said miserably.

Behind them, a soft moan announced Sam was awake.

FIFTEEN

"**W**here am I?" Sam asked thickly as he pushed himself to a sitting position.

"Sam? Are you all right?" Chloe asked, hurriedly kneeling beside him. "He needs to feed," she said, recognizing his symptoms from the last time she'd seen him unconscious. Her gaze drifted to Ducante. "You don't happen to have any . . . ?"

"What do you think a Bloody without the Mary is, my dear? Of *course* I do."

When he made no move to help, she tried again: "Well, can we get some for Sam?"

Sam squinted his dark, vampire eyes, looking blearily at her. "I'm Sam," and then, "Hey. I . . . I know you. You're . . . you're a hunter who doesn't hunt," he said vaguely.

"Damn it," Ducante muttered, stalking off to commandeer a bag of blood from the freezer.

After Sam had fed, he seemed slightly more together. He tried to answer her questions, but he'd retained very little information from the past few weeks and knew nothing of what happened to him.

In fact, other than knowing *what* he was, he didn't seem to know much of anything, not even what sort of vampire he'd been before waking up on Ducante's floor. He was a blank slate.

It wasn't hard for her to persuade him he was not only in danger, but in danger of doing something completely unforgivable, as well. A bit more persuading, and the idea of feeding directly from humans made him shudder; murder was certainly out of the question. She didn't understand it, but Sam's energy had, for better, or worse, changed completely after Aurelia's intervention.

Mikhail insisted they all stay together; it was the best option given the cards on the table. Aurelia would be in danger as soon as the demons were raised. And those looking to bring Pan and Damonos back had likely realized what they'd need, and were already searching for her.

Aurelia quickly agreed, offering up her empty house.

Sam seemed quite relieved by the idea; his new energy left him unsure. He lingered next to Chloe whenever possible, as if reassured by the one person he could somewhat recognize.

In an odd twist of symmetry, Aurelia seemed to latch on to Mikhail. Despite his gruff exterior, something about him seemed to calm her. Or maybe she found him attractive, even with the scars and tattoos. Chloe didn't know.

≥∞

The first day, Mikhail insisted he go speak with Rus and Alex, as well as set up passable excuses for Aurelia and Chloe's absence from school. Ordinarily, Chloe would have simply withdrawn, but in order to avoid any trace of suspicion, one of them was diagnosed with appendicitis while the other claimed family emergency.

"Which is which?" Aurelia hissed. They'd spent much of the

day sitting on the couch, watching movies on the large TV that dominated the living room. Aurelia hadn't seen a need to change out of her pajamas, but when Mikhail entered, she quickly threw a black fleece blanket over herself. "When we get back, how do we know who used what excuse?"

Chloe raised an eyebrow and gave Aurelia a sidelong glance. She was pressed as far back into the cushions as possible so that her powers wouldn't disrupt the technology. The Made-for-TV movie playing in front of them involved a woman finding out her husband was leading a double life. The irony was not lost on her. "It won't matter. You're a thought-weaver, remember?" She didn't bother mentioning that Aurelia might not be *going* back—the supernatural didn't often mingle with the human world.

From the kitchen, Mikhail chuckled. Aurelia's cheeks burned.

"Whatever," she mumbled. And then, seeming genuinely regretful, she added, "This might ruin your chances, you know."

"Ruin my chances for what?" Chloe asked, watching as the woman on the screen entered the house where her husband was hiding his real identity.

"Spring Fling Queen," Aurelia replied, clearly exasperated. "Duh."

This warranted an actual laugh from Chloe. She pulled her gaze away from the TV, giving the girl an incredulous look. "*That's* what you're worried about?"

Aurelia shrugged. "Whatever. If it's the end of the world, I at least want Corinne to experience some sort of suffering before it happens."

In the kitchen, there was a strangled sort of chuckle as Mikhail choked on his sandwich.

❧

"We don't know the ritual," Mikhail said darkly. "How can we disrupt something we have no way of anticipating?"

Chloe sighed, shaking her head slowly. Aurelia had gone to bed, and Sam was in the basement. A side effect of his reprogramming was a particular bashfulness when it came to his feeding habits. Ducante had delivered a cooler full of hospital blood bags, along with a note detailing how his regular customers were billed and how, for a home delivery, the price would be doubled. Sam had glanced at the note, collected the cooler, and retreated down the stairs. A fact Chloe, for one, was pleased with.

"Our best bet is to kill them as quickly as possible, before they regain their powers," Mikhail was saying, pulling her back into the present. "Then we can focus on finding the person who's so hell-bent on bringing these bastards back."

"There's going to be so many people around," Chloe said quietly. "Aurelia, Sam . . ."

Mikhail fixed her with a hard stare. "People will run at the first sign of commotion. They aren't *that* stupid; flight or fight is a basic survival instinct. As for Aurelia and Sam, they don't need to be there."

Chloe frowned. "Yes, they do."

"How would that help anything? Aurelia hardly knows how to use her powers, much less use them offensively. And Sam . . . if he's part of all this, I see no reason why we'd want to bring him closer to the situation."

Chloe bowed her head, rubbing her temples. The icy chrome and stark, vacant colors of the house were already starting to give her a headache, and it was only day one. "Aurelia has to go. It's her . . . well, it's her Spring Fling. The last thing she'll be able to enjoy while she's completely human, you know? Before she has to really be a part of this world. And we need her to get you into the dance. You're not exactly a student at Molton."

Her brother frowned. "We do *not* need her to get into the dance." He paused, and then sighed. "But I suppose her being there wouldn't hurt anything. She can run just as well as everyone else."

For a moment, Chloe toyed with the idea of mentioning Aurelia's sub-par performance in gym class, but decided it wouldn't favor her argument any. Instead, she elected to change the subject. "And Sam will come with me."

"Chloe—"

"No. No, he can be useful—he can look out for anything unusual. If he's part of it, don't you think we'd notice when he starts to react to something? And we can't leave him here, whoever's after him could just come pluck him up if he's not protected."

Mikhail shook his head in frustration. "We wouldn't leave him *here*. He could stay with Alex, or Rus, maybe. They'll be sitting on the sidelines with the Ways."

An odd, fuzzy feeling washed over her. Dare she call it smug? "He can't stay with them."

"You're being ridiculous."

"What would they do to him if something went wrong?" she demanded, rising from the couch. "He doesn't deserve that kind of treatment and—"

"Christ, Chloe, what is your fascination with this vampire?" Mikhail hissed, trying to keep his voice low. "I'm all for compassion, but don't you think you're getting a little out of control? He's still just—"

"Someone I saved. Twice," she interjected. She didn't know why she felt so strongly about Sam—it might have had something to do with his new, puppy-dog-esque demeanor—but she felt connected somehow, responsible for him. She didn't know how to explain that, though, especially with Mikhail on the offensive. All the thoughts she'd had about him being the one person she'd be able to talk to were quickly evaporating.

Mikhail said nothing in response.

Chloe shook her head. "I need to get out of this house," she mumbled.

"Is that really the best—"

"Just to get some clothes and stuff," she snapped, crossing her arms over her chest. "Or is that not the best decision either?"

He sighed. "Fine. Don't be gone long."

With that, she was out of the house and away. It only took a moment before she stood at the edge of her yard. The little ivy-covered house was almost entirely hidden in the darkness. She took a deep breath, closing her eyes, her heart racing from the exertion. It felt nice to be somewhere familiar, somewhere that, just a few weeks ago, had been a perfectly comfortable home, free of anything abnormal.

She took another deep, slow breath. The late night breeze brushed across her face. As she began to exhale, she heard it: a rustling in the nearby bushes too great for the wind to have caused. She spun, knife already in hand.

A particularly fat possum paused to stare at her with its beady little eyes.

"You're mighty jumpy tonight, Princess."

She whipped back around: sure enough, there he was, standing between her and her house. Josef. Her grip on the knife tightened.

"I didn't think you'd come back here," he offered lightly.

"Which is why you were here waiting," she said icily.

He shrugged. He was dressed more casually than the last time she'd seen him: dark jacket over a dark shirt and pants. Night-time camouflage. "It didn't hurt to try. I found you, didn't I?"

She gritted her teeth, squeezing the knife once, twice. Breathe in, breathe out. "I don't know if that decision was in your best interest."

"Whoa now, Princess," he protested, holding his hands up defensively. "Where is this hostility coming from?"

"Oh, I don't know," she said, a chill in her voice, "Maybe it's because you drugged me. Why are you here? Aren't you done being Ducante's lackey?"

Josef opened his mouth and then shut it quickly, squaring his jaw. "Is that what you think?" His tone was different now. Heavier.

"That's what I *know*," she replied forcefully. "Your job is done. I'm taking care of this whole mess come Saturday, so—"

"That's why I'm here," he said, taking a quick step forward. Too quick—vampire quick. She pulled the knife up, but he pushed her hand away with more force than he'd ever displayed around her. "Don't go on Saturday."

She recoiled at his touch. "And let the world go to hell? No, thanks."

"I'm serious, Chloe. Don't go," he repeated, trying to hold her gaze with his own.

A surge of anger went through her. She reached out and shoved him—hard, with a push of power behind it. He stumbled back a step. "Did Ducante put you up to this? Because he should know by now that we're his best shot. And for the love of God, he can tell me himself if he's so—"

"Ducante didn't send me," Josef growled. He took a step forward, bringing them closer together again.

"Then why are you here?" she shouted, standing her ground. Birds roosting in a nearby tree took off in startled flight

Josef closed the gap between them, grasping her shoulders with steel trap strength. Her heart was hammering in her throat;

she knew better than to move. It would only end in a dislocated shoulder or a snapped arm.

"You really don't get it," he hissed. His face was so close to hers, but his expression—distorted and twisted with rage and frustration—frightened her. "It will not end well for you if you go. Don't. Go."

Chloe narrowed her eyes as she glared into his unchanging expression. "No."

He let out a frustrated growl and shoved her away from him. She stumbled before regaining her balance. He'd already taken several steps away and stood with his back to her, his arms crossed. His head lifted toward the star-studded sky. "You really think you can stop them. You don't understand anything," he said softly.

The tone of his voice, so defeated and hard, shocked her almost as much as his expression had. "Josef . . ."

He turned to face her, his posture tense, expression guarded. She'd never seen him like this.

"There are forces at play you couldn't understand," he said vaguely, looking at her but also through her. "You will do as you choose. I would just prefer you not end up dead."

"If you don't want me to end up dead, maybe you should make your messages less cryptic."

He turned to leave. She opened her mouth to say something, anything, but she was at an absolute loss. He paused, looking over his shoulder at her.

"And just so I don't cause any more problems, I'll say it again: Ducante did not send me." With that, he was gone, leaving nothing more than a patch of quaking bushes in his wake.

❧

Chloe was shaking. It had taken definite effort to gather her clothing instead of going after Josef. When she reappeared at Aurelia's, she stayed crouched in the bushes, her head in her hands.

Josef was right: there was so much she didn't understand.

When she was absolutely sure everyone was either asleep or otherwise occupied, she crept into the house. Once she'd made it to her assigned room—the cold, chrome and leather office—she flung herself onto the couch and didn't move.

She spent the next day in honor of Sam, not emerging from her room until late in the afternoon. She wrangled a sandwich from the refrigerator and nodded to Aurelia and Mikhail, deep in conversation in the living room, before returning to seclusion.

The second time she decided to leave her self-imposed captivity, it was late at night. She'd started to feel dizzy chasing her own thoughts around the same four walls and needed a change.

She paced the kitchen five times before she realized Sam was sitting in the living room.

"Hello," he said vaguely, tearing his eyes away from the nothingness he'd been staring at.

"Hi, Sam," she replied with a sigh. For a moment, she wished the hard, emotionally distant Sam was still in existence. She wasn't sure she was in a place to deal with his new brand of vulnerable honesty.

"What have you been doing?" he asked, cocking his head to the side. "I could hear your heart beating fast."

Chloe blinked in surprise. Of course he could hear her; vampires relied on their senses. She supposed she just never realized how much. "I . . . I've just been thinking. About life. And it's shortcomings." Though she was specifically thinking of the life of a Naimei, she figured this sounded much more philosophical and acceptable to Sam, who was still living under the impression she and Mikhail were witches.

"That's funny," Sam said, his voice distant, "I was thinking the same thing about death."

Chloe frowned as she carefully selected a seat on one of the ultra-modern, black chairs. "Why were you thinking about that?"

"Because that's what's happening at the end of the week, right?" He turned his head ever so slightly to look at her. "To me. To everyone. That's why everyone's heart is beating fast."

She clenched her jaw to stave off a shiver. "No," she answered firmly, "No, that's not going to happen to anyone. Although, to be fair, you're already dead."

"Yes," he said, sounding slightly reassured. He didn't say anything further, and they both lapsed into silence.

Chloe took the opportunity to study him. He was paler than usual. Apparently, the blood Ducante provided was either not enough or not up to par with what he'd been eating before. His expression was blank: it had been that way, more or less, since they'd returned from the bar. Chloe wondered what exactly had happened with Aurelia inside his head.

"They're worried," he offered. "The other two. They wanted to see you today."

"I didn't want to talk to anyone," she said honestly. There was no point lying, it would have been too easy in his current state, and she would have felt downright guilty.

"Why?"

Chloe sighed. "Have you ever felt like maybe you've just been living a very realistic lie? That you thought you understood everything, but you really know nothing in the end?"

After another moment of silence, he answered, "Maybe.

But," he grabbed at his hair in frustration, "I don't remember anything anymore."

"I'm sorry," she offered.

"I don't think they wanted to talk to you," he went on, as if his outburst hadn't happened. "They just wanted to see you."

She shifted in her seat, unsure what to do with this new insight.

"Oh well," he continued, "Maybe it will be better tomorrow."

Chloe stood up, brushing herself off. "Maybe," she agreed. "Goodnight, Sam."

❧

Just as Sam had predicted, things were better the next day. When Chloe came downstairs late in the morning, she was surprised to see all the furniture in the living room pushed to the perimeter. Mikhail and Aurelia were standing in the middle of the space, facing one another.

Neither moved. Then, abruptly, Mikhail cringed—he yelled and raised one arm sharply upward. Aurelia flew back into the couch.

"Hey!" Chloe shouted, stepping forward, her eyes wide.

But Aurelia was laughing from her spot in the cushions. "That was good, right? I got to you from six feet away!"

Mikhail chuckled and nodded. "Yeah, you're getting there. We'll move on to physical fighting soon. Hey, Chloe."

"We've been practicing," Aurelia gushed.

"I figured if Aurelia's going to be at the gardens, she might as well be prepared," Mikhail elaborated as she shuffled into the room. At her expression, he added, "Just in case things don't go as planned."

"I'm getting a lot better. I can control what I do and every-thing!"

"That's . . . good," Chloe said cautiously, sinking to a cross-legged pose on the floor. "What all can you do?"

"A little bit of everything, really," Mikhail said, stretching one arm across his chest. "Rearrange thoughts. Implant new ones."

"Pull up really painful ones and make it so they're all you can think about," Aurelia added with an odd happiness that didn't quite fit her words.

Chloe plucked at a loose fiber in the carpet. "And that works? Offensively?"

Mikhail shrugged. "Yeah. I mean, she can make you remember the worst pain you've ever been in until you feel like you're completely reliving it."

Chloe's arm, now fully healed, gave a phantom ache.

"I'm still not, you know, great, but Mikhail thinks I should focus on becoming well-rounded, so we're going to work on sparing."

"Sparring," Mikhail corrected, retrieving two butter knives from a nearby table. "I figured we'd start safe and work our way up. What do you think, Chloe?"

"I . . . all right. I mean, yeah, I guess that sounds good," she answered. She was surprised her absence yesterday went by unmentioned. In a way, she was grateful for their preoccupation, and yet also felt guilty that they'd been so productive while she did nothing but wallow.

"Then you'll help me demonstrate," Mikhail said, tossing her a knife.

Chloe stared at it for a moment. She worked her hand around the handle and then shook her head, tossing it to Aurelia. "I'll use my own, thanks," she directed to Mikhail, and then, to Aurelia, "The best way to learn is to cut yourself a few times."

Aurelia shook her head slowly. "No wonder everyone at Molton thought you were a badass. That's what's going to get you Spring Fling queen, you know."

Chloe snorted and waved one hand in the hair. Within seconds, her knife had zoomed down the stairs, the handle landing

189

in her hand. She preferred not to use her powers for menial tasks, but maybe that was why more complicated ones tired her so much. Already, her heart thrummed in her chest, though it was aided by adrenaline as she swapped places with Aurelia and stood in the center of the room.

Mikhail lunged first. He was checking his speed; there was no power behind it. He was only slightly faster than a human, and she'd been expecting much more. She dove aside. He turned, lashing out at her with his blade. She regained her balance just in time to parry, but he caught the motion and flipped the knife easily out of her hand. The physical blow she aimed at his solar plexus was turned against her and she found herself staring at the ceiling, her own knife pressed to her throat.

"Whoa," Aurelia breathed.

They sparred three more times, each fight increasing in intensity, before addressing the human at the side of the room. Panting, Chloe retreated to the kitchen for water as Mikhail explained to Aurelia that any supernatural she was likely to face would fight harder and faster than what she'd just seen.

If it was meant as a deterrent, it didn't work. Aurelia seemed to have been seized by a new determination at his words, and she gave a grim nod as she took her place in the living room.

Though untrained, Aurelia was not hopeless as a fighter, which was surprising given the physical ability she'd demonstrated in Phys Ed. The work Mikhail had done with her to enhance her powers seemed to give her a limited foresight into their next moves: Chloe and Mikhail took turns putting her through the paces, and she was able to evade most attacks until they increased their speed. But even then, she found a way to twist out of the most forceful takedowns. It was beneficial, Chloe supposed, but the girl had yet to master any physical attacks.

They'd just begun to teach her the most basic offense when Sam emerged from the basement. He lingered on the periphery, watching as Chloe and Mikhail allowed Aurelia to practice attacking without trying to block or dodge.

When they resumed sparring, Sam joined the rotation to help acclimate her to the speed only vampires moved with. He even took a turn fighting Chloe and Mikhail. Chloe had him pinned before it started. She shot a smug look at her brother. He was sporting an angry red mark on his chin where Sam had gotten a good crack in before Mikhail managed to get him on the ground.

He wiped the mark angrily, and after a soft glow, it vanished entirely.

The afternoon faded into night. They all slipped off to their respective rooms, one by one. Mikhail flipped his knife once before sliding it to its place at his belt. He gave Chloe a nod and a grin; it was good to have him back.

ॐ

The next day brought more of the same; and the next, and the next. They'd start with a late morning meal, work until Sam appeared in the afternoon, which marked a second break, and then work until Aurelia was exhausted.

There was little time to talk, which Chloe preferred. Mikhail and Aurelia seemed to get along marvelously; their banter from the first few days had coalesced into true conversation, and neither much noticed the silent third wheel.

Whenever Chloe wasn't fighting, she was spinning Josef's warning in her head. She had yet to tell anyone about it. She could no more burden Aurelia, who still found time to giggle about the dance and the things she'd left behind in high school, than she could face the betrayal that would surely be etched on Mikhail's face. So she said nothing and continued her descent into the background.

❧

On Friday, Mikhail decided that Aurelia, who'd been diligently practicing her knife work with the butter knife, was ready for a real knife. She used a spare of Chloe's; the handle was better suited to a slim grip. Mikhail's knives housed sharp silver blades, but the handles were mostly wrought from thick, worn, animal horns that seemed to mirror the aged scars carved into his hands and arms.

Aurelia managed to cut herself three times by late afternoon. On the third slice—a cut just above the knee sustained in a roll—Sam stood and left the room. Aurelia tried to maintain a sanguine attitude, but her gray eyes were filled with frustration.

Mikhail called a stop to the practice. With a wave of his hand, the furniture flew back into place.

The rest of the afternoon was spent watching light-humored movies. Mikhail and Chloe positioned themselves as far from the TV as possible, as it was prone to flickering with both of them in the room.

Before anyone knew it, it was Saturday.

❧

Chloe twisted and turned in front of the floor to ceiling, black-framed mirror in Aurelia's bathroom. It was large and overly ornate, fitting perfectly with the cold, ultra-modern theme in the rest of the house. She twirled, eyeing the dress she'd retrieved from her closet. The soft, mauve fabric wrapped around her torso in a tight, strapless bodice, ballooning into a bell skirt at the waist.

She looked like a flower.

How appropriate, she thought, tucking a pin into the spirals of hair she'd piled atop her head.

Aurelia had had a dress picked out for months; an elegant floral-print that draped to her knees. Mikhail, perhaps because of Chloe's insistence that Aurelia enjoy one last experience as a human, truly stepped up to the role of date. He'd used some of his powers to coax weeds from the lawn into a beautiful corsage that matched Aurelia's dress perfectly.

He'd also spent time perfecting the clothes he and Sam wore. Chloe knew that was a struggle; no one in their family had any great power over domestic magic. So she bit her tongue when she noticed the frayed edges on the dress pants that had once been old jeans.

Mikhail looked pleased with himself. He'd somehow found time to arrange for a car; it was no limo, but the sleek town car seemed just as acceptable to Aurelia. He grinned as he ushered her, Chloe, and Sam into the back.

Chloe took a deep breath as Mikhail slid into the passenger seat and smiled at the driver.

"Greater Molton Botanical Gardens, please," he requested smoothly.

Somewhere in her throat, Chloe's heart was pounding for a reason that had nothing to do with using her powers. As they'd exited the house, she'd had the distinct feeling she was being watched.

SIXTEEN

They went over their plan in the car after Mikhail made it known that, thanks to a little magic he and Aurelia had cooked up, the driver would have no memory of the ride. He was in the middle of planning his dream vacation—a very, very elaborate dream vacation.

They knew the ritual relied on the equinox, so it made sense that whatever was going to happen would probably take place at midnight. They had no idea *where* it would take place, though: presumably, it would be in an area that wasn't densely populated. Whether they needed bodies or not, there was no reason for two powerless demons to reemerge in a sea of human teenagers.

When they arrived at 10 p.m.—Aurelia had warned that any earlier would make them absolute pariahs—they made a few laps around the premises. The gardens were expansive, and, Chloe had to admit, beautiful. They housed every flower that was feasibly possible in Molton's fickle temperatures, and even some that were not. Intricate paths wound through the flora, stemming from the center area where the dance was located.

Tiny strings of fairy lights led the way to the faux wood dance floor. An audience of delicate, white patio furniture sat in clusters nearby. Chloe thought the furniture looked much too elegant for a high school dance, but at the joy on Aurelia's face, she held her tongue. The DJ, who was truly horrendous, was playing on a small, raised platform near one of the outbuildings. There were several, all connected by a portico—hung thick with ivy—that led to an elaborate fountain.

Chloe and Mikhail had decided they'd use Sam as a compass; the second he started to act odd, they'd follow him, detain him, and stop whoever was attempting to raise the demons.

At least, that's how they hoped the plan would go.

"Nothing's happening," Sam hissed in Chloe's ear as he spun her around to the beat of some new pop hit.

It was already 11:19 according to the tall, wrought-iron clock standing near the rose garden on the far side of the dance floor. It was supposedly a marker for those who wanted to venture into the prize of the gardens—the hedge maze. It was far from large, but had been cultivated for decades. The walls were quite high.

Chloe sighed, sending out another small burst of power. The results, save for Sam, were frustratingly human.

"It's not time yet, Sam," she hissed back.

"This is taking forever," he complained.

Chloe rolled her eyes, swaying to the music.

Several couples away, Mikhail was laughing as he spun Aurelia around and around in circles. He looked happier than Chloe was used to seeing him, and Aurelia's smile was, if possible, beyond ear-to-ear. She made a mental note to talk to him about what he was doing, playing with the heart of a human girl.

But not tonight, she thought.

Things were going much too well. Aurelia not only seemed to be having a good time, she was commanding the attention of the room. People seemed to think Mikhail was fairly attractive—perhaps because he'd once again gone out of his way to hide his tattoos—and together, they may as well have been on display in the center of the fountain for all the attention they garnered.

Sam received his fair share of looks, too, as did Chloe; though some of hers were far from pleasant.

Corinne had made it clear she wasn't pleased by Chloe and Aurelia's reappearance after a week's absence from school. She'd made loud remarks about their attire to those she stood near; namely, her bulky, football-player date, Heather—on the arm of a similar footballer—and her brother, complete with a skinny blonde of his own. Even now, Chloe could occasionally hear raucous laughter from across the dance floor.

Corinne's outbursts picked up more and more as the night drew on. Especially after two bored-looking chaperones set up a table under the ivy-covered portico, just outside the bathrooms. Aurelia explained it was to tally the votes for Spring Fling king and queen. Traditionally, the couple was announced just before midnight so they could spend the last hour as royalty.

"Hear that, Chloe?" Mikhail said, prodding her in the side. "You could be royalty while you slay some ancient demons."

Sam watched in curious confusion as Chloe swatted her brother's hand away. "Shut up. No way it's me. High school and I were never meant to be."

Yet, as fewer and fewer students emerged, laughing, from the voting table, Chloe felt her heart speed up. She couldn't tell if it was because she dreaded the result, or if she secretly wanted the title.

Another dreadful pop song was drawing to a close, but nothing followed it. A murmur ran through the crowd. One of the bored chaperones, a science teacher Chloe vaguely recognized, stepped onto the DJ's platform, blocking the soundboard, a microphone in his hand.

The waiting students fell silent faster than they ever had in class.

"Ladies and gentlemen," he began with forced enthusiasm, "It's the moment you've been waiting for. The votes are in, and it's time to announce the Spring Fling king and queen!"

A cheer erupted from the crowd. Chloe felt Sam flinch at the unexpected noise.

The teacher began a small speech about the importance of the position and what it meant to win, but at the impatient expressions etched on every student in attendance, he stopped rather abruptly. "Ah. As I was saying, with over half the votes, the title of Spring Fling king goes to . . ." he flipped open a rumpled piece of a scrap paper, "Jared Palgrave!"

Chloe glanced around the room. The thick-set boy Corinne had come with was accepting congratulations from those nearby. Derek slapped him hard on the back. Corinne squealed as she gave him a kiss on the cheek and then pushed him toward the stage.

Half the crowd applauded as he mounted the platform, though some looked particularly glum. If he'd won as king, there was little doubt Corinne would be queen; Aurelia looked positively crestfallen.

"All right, all right!" the teacher snapped, as if the crowd was out of control. Jared Palgrave, who'd taken his place on the platform, raised his hands to quiet his subjects. Chloe saw him give Corinne a wink.

"And now," the teacher said more loudly. The crowd immediately became silent. "The Spring Fling queen." He squinted down at the paper in his hands, and read: "Cor. . . I'm sorry. *Chloe* Moraine."

Silence reigned for the length of a heartbeat.

"Are you *kidding me?*" Corinne shouted

The students broke into applause. There was a definite whooping noise from Aurelia, a whistle from Mikhail. Across the dance floor, Roger seemed to be celebrating enthusiastically, much to the dismay of his shy-looking date.

Chloe felt a push on the small of her back. Sam was ushering her toward the platform. Derek was standing near the stage, shouting the improbability of it all to the teacher, who seemed to pay him no mind. Chloe edged around him and accepted the crown, giving a weak smile to Jared Palgrave.

"All right, now, shake hands! Give these people some photo opportunities."

She extended her hand. A dark look crossed Jared's face; he was either upset his date wasn't queen, or he'd heard from Derek what she'd done on *their* first meeting. Maybe both. When he gripped her hand, it was like a vice; she could see him grit his teeth as he tightened his hand around her fingers.

She smiled serenely back at him; it wouldn't take much power to break his hand, but that would cause too much of a scene. Instead, she clenched her fingers, using just enough force for him to feel. As a panicked expression formed on his features, she felt a sadistic sort of satisfaction settle somewhere in her stomach.

"Let's give them a round of applause," the teacher was continuing, not that the crowd had ever gone silent.

Chloe dredged up a smile from somewhere deep, deep down, and even offered a small wave of thanks while Jared investigated his hand for potential damage. She spotted Aurelia, laughing at Corinne's scorned expression. Mikhail offered her two thumbs up; even Sam managed a small smirk. But they weren't what held her focus; behind the cheering group of students, in the rose bushes that rimmed the edge of the dance floor, she'd caught a flash of movement, in a very familiar dark jacket.

After ascertaining his hand was intact, Jared continued waving, soaking in the attention more than Chloe ever cared to. She was the first to dismount the stage. She wanted to run to the rose bushes, to search for the familiar vampire, but her progress was immediately halted by a gaggle of students rushing to congratulate her. She pushed out a flash of power, but it was useless. The number of humans surrounding her made it impossible to get a clear read on anything.

The crowd didn't get any better when she reached Sam, and especially not once the music started. Everyone wanted to dance near the Spring Fling queen, and the pounding techno beats only encouraged them. Any hope she had of following Josef—of finding out why he'd come—was lost by the second song.

Sam swung her around to the music. She would politely shout "Thank you," and "That was nice, thanks," over his shoulder without ever having to truly interact with students whose names she barely knew. As the song drew to a close, he pulled away, shaking his head.

Chloe instantly became motionless. "Is it . . . ?"

"No," he scowled, "Just too many humans. I need some air."

"But, Sam," she asked innocently, "Who will I dance with?"

He rolled his eyes before pushing his way through the onlookers toward the ivy-covered portico. Mikhail caught Chloe's gaze; she gave a minute shake of her head, tapping just below her eye as surreptitiously as possible. He nodded and then grinned at Aurelia, swinging her around so they could keep a better eye on where Sam had gone.

She ended up dancing next to Roger and his awkward date, who did little more than sway out of time and in place.

Even so, her dancing was a slight improvement over Roger's, whose entire repertoire seemed to come from the early 80's. She found herself laughing as the song ended, so preoccupied that she didn't notice anyone approaching until they reached out to grab her elbow.

When she spun around, she expected to see another student she barely recognized. Or worse, one of Corinne's cronies: she'd heard them angrily shouting for a recount as she'd left the stage. But instead, it was a tall boy with tousled hair and dark, dark eyes.

Vampire eyes.

"What are you doing here?" she whispered. He was dressed much the same as he'd been the night they'd watched the Cuckoo's Nest play; a debonair flair in the atmosphere of the dance. A good few people had torn their gaze from Chloe to stare at him.

"Why, asking for this dance, of course," he replied with a small smile, holding his hands up in a waltz posture.

Chloe frowned and made a quick scan of the room. Nothing unusual was happening yet; they still had time before midnight. A few couples away, Mikhail was frowning. "Fine," she said quickly, shifting to shield her new partner from view. "Fine."

Josef grabbed her hands, pulling her close. Her dancing experience was limited to none; she got by mostly on the reflexes and balance she'd developed from hunting. Josef, however, seemed to know exactly what he was doing. He didn't dawdle with the box-step swaying most of the couples around them were demonstrating, but instead, spun her expertly around the dance floor, drawing even more stares. She could hear whispers starting anew as they worked their way around the area.

"You look marvelous tonight, Princess," he said softly, looking down at her. "I suppose this is the only time I can call you that and be accurate."

"I'm a queen tonight, actually," she corrected. "And you still haven't answered my question."

"Maybe I just wanted my chance to dance with royalty," he quipped, dipping her halfway to the ground before pulling her effortlessly back up.

"Josef," she said sharply, both because of his answer and the dip. "Why are you here? Did Ducante send you?"

"Ducante does not send me anywhere," he answered dully, spinning her away from him before pulling her back in. "I thought I explained that to you during our last encounter."

Chloe caught sight of Mikhail and Aurelia over Josef's shoulder; Aurelia was standing on her tiptoes, whispering something to a vexed-looking Mikhail. "Then why did you come here? You said coming wouldn't end well. I heard that much."

"For *you*," Josef added, quickly and ominously. "Coming here wouldn't end well for *you*. I'm here because . . . well, let's not spoil the night with that. I'm here because I'm here, and while I'm here, I'll warn you."

"Warn me about what?" she whispered.

"You need to run," he said, leaning down to whisper in her ear. "Get those that are with you, and run."

She pulled back from him sharply. "I . . . I can't do that. We have a plan. We—"

"Shh," Josef demanded, placing one finger against her lips as he pulled her toward him. She wondered dimly if he could feel the shiver that went down her spine. "Chloe, you have to listen to me. You may yet find vengeance on the person responsible for this—but it won't happen tonight. Not if you plan to survive."

"Why are you telling me this? How do you even *know* this?" she demanded, pulling his hand away from her mouth.

He frowned. There was an emotion burning somewhere

behind the darkness of his eyes: she thought she recognized it as remorse, mixed with something else. "Because, I—"

Abruptly, he was pulled away from her. She let out a small yelp before realizing it was Mikhail's doing.

"Excuse me," Mikhail said through clenched teeth, "But who the hell are you?"

"Chloe, I'm sorry," Aurelia whimpered from his elbow. "I . . . I didn't know he was a . . . a . . ." Her teeth began to chatter as she looked up at Josef, like she was seeing a true monster for the first time.

Chloe wanted to point out that Josef was no different than Sam, whom she'd shared a roof with for the last week, but the others were already talking.

"That's kind of a rude way to ask for a name, isn't it?" Josef said, crossing his arms over his chest.

"Sorry," Mikhail said in a way that was far from apologetic. "I like to keep tabs on the vampires trying to cozy up to my sister."

Josef raised an eyebrow. "I hardly think it's my fault she didn't choose to tell you. Maybe there are some personal problems you should be working out."

Mikhail took a menacing step forward, but Chloe stuck her arm out, slipping between the two of them. "Stop it! Stop it. Josef knows Ducante. He's been . . . he's been, uh, helping."

The look of utter rage Mikhail had been fixing on Josef turned toward her. "*What?* He's been hanging around and . . . and you didn't think to tell anyone? What does he know?"

"He just . . . look, I thought he was working for Ducante. It wasn't a big deal because Ducante was out of the picture; he wasn't the bad guy and—"

"You didn't think to mention that a *vampire* you thought was working for a *demon* took an interest in your personal life? How long has this been going on?"

"I . . . I don't know, a few weeks, but . . . it's not . . . why are you making such a big deal out of this? And why is every-one acting like being a vampire is the end all, here? Sam's been living with us for a week and no one seemed to care!" she shouted, balling her fists in frustration.

Mikhail took a step closer, lowering his voice to a hiss. "Let me just remind you, Chloe, that a month ago, you were killing any vampire that crossed your path. So pardon me if I don't find you the best spokesperson for their rights." He narrowed his eyes. "And really, how stupid can you be? He just conveniently shows up before midnight? To what, *woo you?* He's obviously part of this!"

Chloe stumbled as Josef shunted her out of the way. Aurelia clasped her hands over her mouth, covering a small shriek; he stood inches from Mikhail, his fangs bared. "If you have accusa-tions to hurl," he snarled, "say them to my face."

"Fine," Mikhail spat. "I don't see how you can be here, being what you are, and not be a part of this whole damn thing."

Josef gritted his teeth. "You might be right, Naimei, but I'm definitely not the one you're searching for tonight. And I'm hardly the one you should be concerned with now." His eyes slid to Chloe's, and for a moment, the anger diminished. "Chloe, please."

Mikhail shoved Josef hard in the chest. It must have had some power behind it, because the vampire stumbled a step before regaining his balance. "You have no business talking to her."

"The hell I don't!" Josef growled.

Chloe stepped forward to argue for herself. But no sooner had the words left Josef's lips than a blood-curdling scream pierced the night air.

"What time is it?" Mikhail demanded.

"Where's Sam?" Chloe shouted.

She heard a loud curse and was buffeted by a sudden gust of wind; Josef had taken advantage of the confusion to take off at full speed. But to her utter confusion, he ran in the opposite direction of the scream.

Mikhail cursed and moved toward the portico. Chloe grabbed his shoulder and pulled him back.

Run. Take those with you and run . . . , Josef's words echoed in her head.

"No. No! Stop! Take her and get out of here," Chloe shouted, shoving him back and pointing at Aurelia.

"I . . . what about . . . ?" Mikhail began, pushing Aurelia toward the line of rose bushes.

"I'm getting Sam and taking care of this!" Chloe yelled, turning to the portico. "We'll meet somewhere safe!"

She didn't hear Mikhail's reply as she took off, moving as fast as she dared in the scattering crowd.

She raced past the outbuildings toward the large crowd gathering around the magnificent fountain. She pushed her way through, skidding to a halt in front of the spouting sculpture. A gasp caught in her throat.

Sam stood in the middle of the fountain, under the spray of water, his expression glazed. He was mumbling the same strange language he had in the bar. Chloe felt fear lance through her. Somehow, he'd managed to wrestle both Corinne and Derek into the water with him. He held them pinned to his chest, one arm snaked across both their necks. He was undoubtedly using all his available vampire strength to restrain them: Derek was kicking, threatening, cursing, but Sam didn't budge. Corinne seemed resigned, tears smudging her mascara as they streamed down her face.

Chloe barely had a moment to dive forward, shouting his name, before he acted; flipping a knife up with his free hand, he dragged it in a deep line across his arm before pulling it back across Corinne and Derek's throats.

With a sickening gurgle from Corinne and a wheeze from Derek, the three collapsed into the reddening waters just as Chloe reached them.

She splashed into the fountain, trying to ignore the growing amount of blood. Screams sounded from all sides as the crowd dispersed in terror, smashing into those too panicked to move, retreating from the fountain with the force of a tide rushing out to sea. She lunged into the water, pulling the vampire up by his sopping-wet shirt.

"Sam!" she shouted, trying to shake him. He wasn't moving. "Sam! We have to get out of here . . ."

Was that all there was to the ritual? Was Sam, the very person who'd been under their noses the entire time, the person responsible? And would the demons be returning now, in this fountain? She didn't want to wait to find out; she wrapped one arm around his torso, heaving him out of the water and onto the stonework.

"That's him, that's him. The psycho . . ." students were shouting, pointing at the sopping heap of a vampire.

Sam sputtered weakly. His eyes fluttered open a fraction of an inch.

"Chl . . . wha . . . ?"

Heather was shrieking, her shrill voice carrying over the crowd. "She brought him here. It's her fault. She—" The end of her sentence was cut off by the loud chiming of the hedge maze clock.

It was midnight.

Chloe could hear the water behind her begin to sizzle. She squeezed her eyes shut, mouthing words to the strongest spell she could think of. Throwing one arm out, she tossed the majority of people left in the area backward, knocking them from their feet.

She prayed that keeping them out of sight was enough to keep them safe. Slowly, she turned to face whatever was about to emerge from the fountain.

SEVENTEEN

C hloe had seen a lot of horrible things: unusual sights, bloody sights, horrific sights. But this . . . *this* was truly disturbing.

The people that emerged from the fountain *were* people, but they were not human. They didn't move like humans, twisting and contorting in ways that should have been impossible. Bloody water covered them, dripping from their lifeless, broken bodies as they scrambled to their feet.

They opened their eyes. Brilliant red had replaced the human colors. She'd only seen one other person with eyes like that, and his paled in comparison to these. Corinne blinked. She narrowed her gaze as she looked around, and then opened her mouth. Blood spilled out, leaking down her chin and onto the petal-pink dress she'd worn to the dance. Crimson drops stuck between her over-sharp teeth as she let out a cackle.

Chloe heard Heather scream.

Corinne scanned the room, fixing her gaze on Chloe. A wide, sadistic grin spread across her face. "'I've been thinking about life. And it's shortcomings,'" she mocked.

Chloe froze, her hand on the knife hidden under the hem of her dress. How had she known about that last conversation with Sam?

Corinne tilted her head to the side, taking on a deeper voice. "'That's funny. I've been thinking about death.'"

"Wha . . . what?" Chloe stammered.

"Did you think his life had been his own these last weeks?" Derek hissed. He was investigating his burly arms. Unlike Corinne, he wasn't as dramatic about getting rid of the blood in his mouth. It oozed from between his lips as he spoke.

Corinne shrieked with laughter. Her blonde waves had been dyed a grotesque pink by the bloodied water and bounced around her face like errant pieces of her dress. She lunged forward; Chloe sank into a fighting stance, but the girl grabbed Sam, hauling him up by the back of his neck until he dangled a solid foot above the ground. He let out a moan of protest.

"Patience, Pan," chided Derek/Damonos.

Pan traced her tongue up Sam's neck. Her too-sharp teeth rested over the place a pulse would have been if he'd had one. Sam's eyelids fluttered.

"No!" Chloe shouted.

The word slipped out before she even knew what she was doing. Pan's gaze jerked up and she let Sam drop to the ground. She licked her lips in a satisfied way. "Too true, too true!" she squealed. "I'm sure you taste much better. Much more *alive*."

She hurtled over the wall of the fountain, faster than any vampire. Faster than Ducante. Chloe made a move to dodge, but she was too slow.

Pan's arm darted out, her hand wrapping in Chloe's hair. Chloe screamed as some of the pins pulled loose, grazing against her scalp and tugging out a few pieces of hair. The demon yanked backward and Chloe toppled over, staring up at the ivy-covered ceiling.

"Pan," Damonos said sharply, vaulting out of the fountain. "Careful with this one. She is more powerful than she looks."

"Damn right," Chloe muttered, twisting her body up as quickly as possible. Though Pan was still holding on, it put her in a position to drag her knife across the girl's face. She shrieked and let go, but no sooner had Chloe gained her freedom than she lost it again. She'd woefully under-estimated the speed Damonos possessed, even in Derek's burly body.

In an instant, he'd seized the front of her dress and smashed her against the wall of one of the stone outbuildings. She felt several of her ribs crack and clamped her teeth down hard so she wouldn't cry out. He released her and she slid down the wall, the rough stones tearing through her skin.

Damonos jumped back, allowing Pan to step forward. Her face was healing; slower than the rate of a vampire, certainly, but still healing. She let out a shrill laugh and dove toward Chloe again.

This time, she was ready. She rolled aside at just the right moment and heard a satisfying crunch as the demon's skull made contact with the stone. She had her feet under her quick as a flash, and before Pan had even recoiled, shaking her head experimentally, Chloe was running away from the fountain.

Damonos lunged out to wrap a hand around her left arm. She felt the bones snap as he tightened his grip. She screamed.

He gave a harsh tug backward and, for the second time, she found herself on her back. He pulled her uncomfortably into a half upright pose, her broken arm in his grip, her knife hand crushed under his boot.

"I want to make her *scream*," Pan growled, storming onto the scene. Her neck had an odd bend to it, but somehow, she was still standing. Still walking.

They'll be harder to kill than we thought, Chloe thought dully, realizing how stupidly rational the idea was. Her broken arm was starting to go numb and she was almost thankful for the odd hold he had her in.

The demon girl wrenched the knife from her hand and traced a line along Chloe's face. She felt tiny pricks of blood bloom to the surface and grimaced. Pan let out a low, frustrated growl, digging the knife into Chloe's chest just above the mauve fabric. It cut through the skin easily, grinding into her sternum, sending white-hot sparks of pain shooting through her core.

Each twist of the knife scraped against her bone like nails on a chalkboard, sending sickening waves of vibration that were worse than the pain. Was this what it felt like to die? To be on the other end of the hunter's blade? She could feel the dark, sickly aura pouring off the demons and scrunched her eyes closed. *Please*, she thought. *Make it quick.*

Nothing happened.

She opened her eyes cautiously. Pan still stood over her, but the rage had subsided from her face. She wasn't fixing Chloe with a hard glare anymore, but rather, stared into the distance.

"He calls us," Damonos said robotically.

Pan let out another horrific growl. She hissed something in the sickening language Sam had been murmuring and let the knife drop. Chloe sucked in a painful breath as the pressure on her chest eased.

Damonos shook his head. "We are called." And just like that, he let go of her arm. She collapsed to the ground with a thud. Renewed pain coursed through her and she whimpered, curling in on herself.

Pan shouted something else and drove a foot into her side. Chloe coughed as the air left her lungs; pain seared through her torso. Pan's fingers entwined in her hair once more, pulling her head up so their eyes locked. "You were lucky, girl. I *will* find you again." She let go with a jerk that smashed Chloe's temple into the ground. Her vision blurred and a fierce headache bloomed, joining the rest of her body's loud protesting.

She shook her head, trying to force her eyes into focus. They stopped swimming just in time for her to watch the demons take off toward the dance floor. Somewhere in the distance, she could hear sirens roaring.

Pan and Damonos were running quickly—too quick for Chloe to overtake, but perhaps not too quick for her to follow. If she could just see who called them, who'd brought them back . . . she took a deep breath, bracing herself against the pain, and stumbled in the direction they'd gone.

Most of the students had already fled. Some were huddled on the far side of the floor, a nervous-looking chaperone standing in front of them. Others hid on the trails within the gardens. Chloe passed several such couples as she ran. Some shrieked as she approached, others called her name or pointed. Her pace was nowhere near as fast as she would have liked; her ribs ached with every step, and she had next to no power to summon. She was an easy target and her quarry was getting farther and farther away.

She could barely make out the darting shapes of the demons in the distance. Soon, she had to guess as she staggered through the garden, her half-hearted attempt at a run long forgotten. Left or right? Straight or turn? Within minutes, the still-twinkling lights above the dance floor shrank to an indistinguishable blur. She'd reached the far edge of the gardens, where the well-tended foliage began to bleed into overrun national forest.

She slowed. The sirens had grown louder, getting closer and closer; she could just make out the blue and red lights bathing the parking lot in a swirling, garish brilliance.

She felt a hand wrap around her upper arm. She screamed and lashed out, kicking her limbs, driving her fist into whatever, whoever, was in front of her. It made contact with something hard—a jaw, maybe, or a nose. A voice cursed and hissed into the darkness, "Christ, Princess, take it easy."

Chloe sucked in a deep, shaking breath. Her left hand was useless; it throbbed where the bone had snapped. "J-Josef?"

"Who else?" he whispered, tugging her under the tall bush he was crouching beneath. "You're hurt. How the hell did you get out of there alive . . . ?"

She gritted her teeth. Tears were welling in her eyes; she hoped Josef's vision wasn't as good as she suspected. "Why are you still here?" she asked, happy to hear that her voice was still even.

"I . . ." he trailed off. She could make out the outline of his face; his jaw was set in a firm line.

"You're part of this, aren't you?" she said sharply, her voice rising. "My brother was right about you!"

She thought she saw him cringe, but couldn't be sure. "Keep your voice down," he hissed.

"This is just some trap!" she cried, shoving him away with her good arm.

"No, Chloe! Stop, please . . ." He reached out, wrapping his hand around her wrist—the broken one.

She shrieked, and he recoiled.

"Damn it!" he shouted, throwing his hands up in frustration. "I'm sorry, I'm sorry!"

"Why are you still here?" she demanded, tired of his games. She needed answers. *Deserved* answers. "Why did you do any of the stuff you did? Poisoning Sam? All of our late night meetings? What the hell was it for?"

She could just barely make out a glint of white from his teeth as he opened his mouth. "I was given two tasks. The first was to ensure the pieces were in place for Pan and Damonos to return."

"Well, you got your wish. Whatever you were saying to distract me worked, they're back and—"

"My second task," Josef said, talking a little more loudly, cutting her off, "Was to find and kill anyone who could be a threat to that return."

Chloe felt her blood run cold. "You . . . you started following me before any of this happened . . . it was after I stopped hunting . . ."

"I didn't want to do the first, but what choice did I have? My life was on the line. My *freedom*, Chloe. I thought I could do just enough to convince him I was completing my assignment." Josef was still talking, as if he hadn't heard her at all. "Then I realized what completing it would mean, and knew I had to stop it. If I could kill a Naimei, I could lead the rest into a revenge attack that would ruin everything and prevent the demons' return." He took a deep breath. "I would escape unscathed. None of the blame would fall on me. I'd be *free*, Chloe, do you understand?"

Her lip quivered. Her back ached where her ribs cracked, and she realized her breath had turned into ragged gasps. Tears were falling freely down her face; the cut on her cheek burned. *No. No, I don't understand.* "But . . . you didn't do it."

"No," he agreed, taking a step closer. "I didn't do it."

"You had plenty of chances," she challenged, pain and adrenaline making her bold. "Even now. You could kill me now."

He said nothing. He simply stared down at her with the same hardened look he'd gotten the last night she'd spoken to him.

"Why? Why didn't you do it?" she asked tersely. "None of this would have happened. No one else would've gotten hurt. Why didn't you kill me?"

In half a heartbeat, he'd closed the remaining gap between them, seizing her upper arms in a tight grip reminiscent of the demons she'd just been fighting. Her head spun—when he opened his mouth, she half expected to see rows of razor-pointed, too-sharp teeth.

"I've been watching you for a long time, Chloe Moraine," he said softly, lowering his face close to hers. His impossibly dark eyes stood out sharply against his light skin, even in the darkness.

Her heart was racing faster than ever. Her body felt heavy. She wanted to run, but it was impossible. Her limbs were made of lead and she was tired. She was *so* tired. Blood pounded in her ears.

"You really are quite beautiful," Josef whispered, before he touched his lips to hers.

The last thing she was aware of was a distant shriek of laughter from the forest. And then she collapsed.

TO BE CONTINUED

ACKNOWLEDGEMENTS

Megan, for always expecting a new chapter each day of work.

Lauren, for being my first reader, editor, and supporter.

My parents, for dealing with having a weird kid who just wanted to sit in her room and write about different worlds and things that go bump in the night.

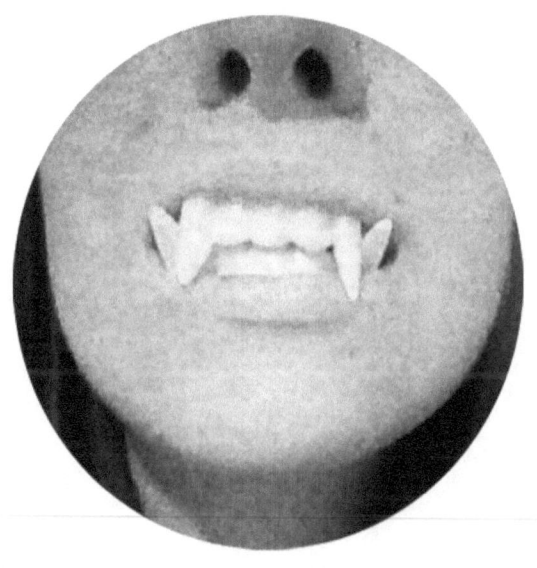

ABOUT THE AUTHOR

Cally Ryanne is a vegetarian in search of the perfect leather jacket. She currently resides in uptown Manhattan, where she lives the glamorous life with three roommates and two adopted cats. Seriously, though. It's a great life.

She (and more of her writings) can be found online at ducanteoriginals.com and twitter @callyryanne.